Strange Sands Suspense 6
St. Augustine

The Black Hourglass

Pamela Poole

Southern Sky Publishing
southernskypublishing.com

This book is fiction. While references are made to actual places, events, and people in history, the characters and incidents within this novel are from the author's imagination. Scripture references are from the CSB version of the Holy Bible.

Cover picture is created with Canva, Craiyon, and Chat GPT online tools
Cover is created on BookBrush

eBook ISBN: 9781956089295
Print ISBN: 9781956089332

Author's Note

This exciting story takes a quick trip from the Lowcountry of South Carolina and back again. The main characters follow a calling to St. Augustine, Florida, where they will set out to solve a mystery with cryptic clues and artifacts hidden in 1688. Some of the historical facts, people, and places are real, but I've woven them into a fictional setting.

The *Strange Sands Suspense* series follows architectural historian Mercedes Annalee Ellison as she investigates historic properties along the South Carolina coast—only to discover that the past often carries spiritual consequences into the present. Routine preservation projects quickly become encounters with hidden passages, ancient vendettas, and unsettling artifacts tied to the unseen realm.

Rooted in a clear Christian worldview, each faith-filled novella blends mystery, suspense, and spiritual warfare with themes of obedience, calling, and trust in God. Clean, gripping, and thought-provoking, *Strange Sands Suspense* is perfect for readers who enjoy inspirational suspense where light confronts darkness and faith makes the difference.

I hope you'll enjoy the Southern Lowcountry ambiance in this series, where moments spent on warm sandy beaches blend with the grains of slipping sand in history's hourglass.

Prologue

Enter through the narrow gate. For the gate is wide and the road broad that leads to destruction, and there are many who go through it.
Matthew 7:13

A simple wooden cross dangled crazily in the sweltering darkness of a family chapel in St. Augustine, Florida. It hung suspended on a long leather cord around the neck of Friar Mateo de la Cruz, who shook off shell fragments and quartz dust from his robe. Coquina was the enduring material used to build the town. The quarry was convenient on nearby Anastasia Island, and it was the perfect material for the underground space at the altar.

He replaced the smooth floor tiles and whispered a prayer over them. When he straightened up and stretched his back, the cross rested peacefully again on rough, earthy brown cotton. Unconsciously, the friar smeared grit across his sweaty brow with the back of his hand. His work in the shadows hid evidence of crimes against the Crown and humanity.

Time was running out for him, as surely as it had run out for Alonzo Alvarez. The bookkeeper had confessed his sins only hours before his murder as he fled town. But those behind his death must repay their borrowed power on borrowed time in the black sand of their symbol, the hourglass. The serpent that wrapped around the middle of it would have them in the end.

As his face crumpled into a grimace of grief over evil deeds that must break God's heart, Friar Mateo de la Cruz sighed deeply. His lungs filled with salty air from the bay. It was heavy with the scent of garden foliage and damp earth. The accountant and his confidants had hidden the evidence he entrusted to the friar, waiting for the fired clay tablet with a message to stand the test of time.

How much time? Only God knew.

The hem of his robe swished over his dusty feet in worn leather sandals. His pace quickened in the darkness. There was much to do under the cover of a sleepy town at night. He had another sealed, timeless vessel to hide where Alonzo Alverez prepared a place under the angel wings. Then he must deliver a message that would mean his death if intercepted.

Back at the friary, a humble candle grew bearded at Friar Mateo's desk. He dipped the quill again, uncertain of the right words to write the most important letter of his life. How many months before it reached the king? Letters lay forgotten for seasons in the governor's house in Havana, where ships left for Spain. Friars had prayed for a reply from Madrid and died of fever before any came.

If the letter made it to Cuba and was entrusted to a fleet captain bound for Spain; if the Atlantic spared the vessel from storms and privateers—there remained the months of waiting for a royal answer to begin its journey. "Six months if the winds favor the trip. A year if they do not," he whispered. "In truth, no help from Spain will come soon enough to save me."

He squeezed his eyes shut and said a prayer inspired by Psalm 31:15. "My times are in thy hand: deliver me from mine enemies, who do evil in thine eyes, Lord."

Eyes hired by the Brotherhood of Shadows watched him, and they silenced poor Alonzo within hours of his confession. The bookkeeper had once been an honest man who naively stumbled into the account records. The threats against his family frightened him. But honest men cannot live under the weight of sin, and the Lord gave him the courage for the act he knew would end his life—stealing the evidence and hiding it, praying justice would someday come.

Alonzo had asked why it had fallen on him to expose dangerous men powered by the occult. Friar Mateo de la Cruz was honest when he told him he did not know. "God's ways are a mystery to me. But He has allowed this in your life, and you surrendered your life to Him. Walk the path of a righteous man."

Justice was unlikely to fall on the powerful Brotherhood in his lifetime, but the evidence would speak when he was gone. The words for King Charles II that had eluded him now flowed onto the linen paper. It was his last message, penned carefully, though he would leave hints and maps in strategic places around the library in the friary. He did not trust the voyage to Spain. But Providence deserved his trust, and the strength of clay, coin, and ink would outlast generations of men.

The friar closed the letter and set down his quill. With great care, he rolled the precious document and wrapped it in parchment. It was ready for the container he would seal, the one that held his letter when presented to the King—or for whoever God willed to find it.

In an hour, the friar hid clues in the library that discerning eyes would understand. He made his way toward the Castillo de San Marcos with the hood of his clean gray robe over his head, blending well into the night shadows. A blanket of humidity muffled his quiet footsteps, and a wicked streak of distant lightning ripped the velvet of the night sky.

The friar wondered if taking Treasury Street was the best route to the fort. Only about six feet wide, the street was built in the common medieval Spanish style, connecting the port to the Royal Treasury.

His nerves tingled with the expectation of danger. There was but one path for a righteous man to take. Alonzo Alvarez had taken it, and so would he. Times were evil. The soldiers in the fort may have collected bribes from his enemy, but there was no one else he could turn to with this letter.

The friar's skin prickled. Was it his imagination, or could he trust his senses that eyes followed him? With a demeanor of serenity he did not feel, he passed through stark shadows cast by sputtering window lanterns. A cat startled him with a sudden, unearthly howl, and his resolve nearly faltered under a jolt of terror. He cast an anxious glance back when he heard the grate of a stone underfoot and caught a fleeting glimpse of a dark cape.

A fellow citizen out late at night? Or was it Alonzo's murderer who ducked between two buildings?

A momentary flash of heat lightning revealed a round-shaped opening in the coquina wall beside him, and before he knew what he was doing, he drew out the glass vial hidden in his robe pocket. The vial was a clean one from the mission's infirmary. It was no longer than a man's hand, with a narrow neck and a rounded lip meant to be sealed with a cork.

The glass was clear, but imperfect from local artisans, bubbled and faintly green from the iron in the sand used to make it.

His letter was nestled inside. Corked and sealed with amber beeswax, the bottle made a watertight container to survive the ocean crossing back to Spain.

At his arm was a place where the uneven blocks were pocked with voids left between the fossilized shells in the stone. A deep natural crevice ran between two slabs with enough space for his purpose.

His heart pounded in his ears as he pressed himself against the rough wall. His fingers pressed the gap and felt loose mortar. Trembling but purposeful, he pushed the sealed glass into the gap to wedge it between the gritty coquina surface. Smearing loosened mortar dust over the opening disguised the bottle from those who now hunted him. The wall looked like any other in a colony built of shell and prayer.

He slipped into the darkness near the fort, where he hoped to deliver the hidden letter before the royal ship left the harbor. Friar Mateo de la Cruz would mislead the man following him. Then he would return near dawn to recover the message in the bottle.

The disquieted cat interrupted the still night again with a nerve-shattering howl. The friar jumped at the noise, then resumed his walk down Treasury Street, whispering fervent prayers. He committed his mission to God's justice, purpose, and plan, asking for another man of God to take it up if he could not fulfill it.

Chapter 1

Jesus Christ is the same yesterday, today, and forever.
Hebrews 13:8

"Wait, Alex. Slow down and start over." Quincy rolled his office chair away from the monitor screen on his desk and picked up his cell phone. He touched the speaker icon to turn it off and put the phone to his ear.

"Get back down here, Quincy, it's the opportunity you asked for," Alex blurted. He was an apprentice from Quincy's last job, and he wanted to work with him again. "You're free to take on the mystery project. The permissions from the city council came through, with the help of the archivist who gave you the information. You're the boss of this research, and while the Catholic Church pays for it, any results are to your professional credit."

Quincy pinched the tension from the muscles in his forehead, letting his mixed emotions roll over him. His heart leaped at this chance, but this was unlike anything he had worked on before. He faced an opponent who was not to be underestimated.

Alex's tone urged him into action. "Quincy, you've taught me to follow intuition and a calling after praying about something. I'm not deaf to a clear *yes* from the Lord. Are you?"

A deep breath fortified Quincy as he straightened into his chair and glanced up at the clock on the wall. He needed to change clothes for his date to take his fiancée out for an early dinner on the island in Sea Pines. "I told Mercedes I'd be free to enjoy the end of the summer here and help her plan the wedding. The timing is bad, that's all. I'll talk to her and call you back as soon as I can."

Quincy made it all the way from the cottage Mercedes rented in Bluffton to the second bridge on Hilton Head Island before she stopped the small talk. "You're distracted tonight, and it's not my new dress. Anything you want to tell me?"

He glanced over at her with a fleeting smile of surprise before he looked to the road ahead. Traffic was getting worse every day as more people found out it was a great place to live and take a vacation. Many were aggressive drivers who were unused to congenial Southern traffic and the slower pace of life lived in Low Country time.

Mercedes looked out over the bridge railing and caught her breath at the view of the sunlight sparkling on the water. "Dolphins!" she exclaimed, leaning toward her window as if to be closer to them.

He grinned. "You can't get to them from here. How many?"

She drew a deep sigh; her eyes locked on the playful animals for the fleeting seconds it took his Mercedes convertible to pass off the bridge onto the island. "Two."

Quincy was uncertain what to say. There was no need, because she had a faraway look and her tone was wistful. "It's unlikely that they're Freedom and Liberty, with so many dolphins here."

She sat back into her leather seat and looked over at him. "I doubt there's any other couple in the world that can say two dolphins brought them back together."

Scenes from that night flashed through his mind, though his eyes remained on the road. His heart raced with an adrenaline surge of the fear he felt for her that night. As he eased the car to a complete stop at the traffic light, he scowled as he turned to her. "It's a miracle that you survived."

Solemnly, she searched his eyes. "Yes," she said. "Jesus deserves the credit, and his ways are not ours. He used two friendly dolphins to answer our prayers."

The light turned green and cars around them started easing forward, so Quincy turned his attention back to the road. Beside him, Mercedes said, "Since that day, we've had a remarkable summer, haven't we? And it's not over yet, is it?"

His head jerked to look at her sharply before he guided his car from a traffic circle toward Sea Pines. "Of course not." He drove a few moments in silence, then added, "Yes, this has been an unforgettable summer, and I don't want to be without you by my side, ever again."

Quincy drew up to the security gate, paid for entry, and eased his car on the way to a restaurant overlooking the Atlantic Ocean. He reached over for his fiancée's hand, on which she wore his engagement ring, and she smiled. But it was a knowing smile. They both understood that he would find a way to answer her question about what he was so distracted about.

"Of course you must go, and I'm going with you," Mercedes said decisively as a server brought salads to their table. Quincy could not respond, since the server lingered to arrange food and light a candle, asking what more he could bring for them. But once he was out of earshot, Quincy took her hand across the table and said a quiet blessing over their food. He then glanced around to see if someone could hear their conversation, and he took a sip of his sparkling water, considering his next words.

"Mercedes, you said you needed a break to plan our wedding. Besides, this isn't like your job. All I have is a hunch that I'm onto something I'm meant to do."

Across the table, the romantic glow from the candle washed over his fiancée's face, softening her tanned features and highlighting strands of her blonde hair. She set down her fork and swallowed a bite of her salad, raising her eyebrows. "In what ways is this different from my job?"

He searched for the right words to answer her, chewing another bite of his steak and gazing out over the ocean. There were so many ways he wanted to respond. She knew little about this project because he did not want her to see the similarity to her last job.

When he remained silent, Mercedes said, "You're leaving out details about this opportunity for your own reasons. I respect that. But it has the stamp of a *calling* all over it, Quincy. You're launching out with sketchy historical information that was given to you, and you say you have a hunch about it. What is a hunch if not guidance? Hasn't intuition been a big part of my job over the past weeks?"

With a sheepish smile, he nodded. "Yes, but I left out the details for a good reason. You've had more spooky stuff haunt you in one summer than most people in this country experience in a lifetime."

They locked eyes before she said, "Now I see. Are you expecting trouble and shielding me, or are you afraid my presence there will attract it? Because you know who I am, Quincy. I tried to escape my calling and became a cautionary tale. Are you doubting that you can live with this?"

There was no challenge in her tone, only an honest question, but he felt a stab of panic. He rushed to reach for her hand across the table. "I can and want to live with it," he insisted. "The truth is, I'm drawn to living through these challenges with you. But in this project, I'm responsible for outcomes. I'm not sure I want to be an archaeologist in the first place, let alone be responsible for your safety."

He blinked, surprised at his own answer. "I mean," he stammered, "well, it was one thing to work as an archaeologist under my dad and as a consultant, but I gave up on archaeology as a career path when I settled down. I don't want a life spent traveling the world, only a life spent here with you."

Mercedes squeezed his hand, and her tone was urgent. "If we marry, you're going to be responsible for my safety around the clock, working or playing, everywhere we are. We should be wary and smart about risks, but we aren't called to live without them. What's that saying? *A ship in harbor is safe, but that's not what ships are made for.* Right? The night Jesus brought us back together—you saved my life. That wasn't your job—you were there to catch a thief."

Quincy nodded. "Not *if* we marry—*when* we marry. And all this is true, but this isn't the place to explain what's on my mind. Let's enjoy dinner together. We'll talk about this later."

After dinner, Quincy drove to Harbour Town, where he and Mercedes strolled hand in hand past the sleek yachts in the marina, the boutiques and restaurants, and the red and white striped lighthouse. Soon, they would be at the end of the pier to enjoy a beautiful view of the sunset.

He wished a decision about his immediate future did not loom before him, and he hated the uncertainty about how that decision would affect his relationship with Mercedes. The setting, the meal, and being with her made him long for peaceful, lazy days ahead to relax from a tough summer schedule and a job he was glad to have behind him.

Instead, he felt restless and uncertain. She had raised points he needed to deal with before putting on his archaeologist hat again and driving back to St. Augustine.

Mercedes leaned into the railing on the pier, looking down into the lapping water at low tide, then off into the western sky. But Quincy's eyes were on her, lingering, noting her silhouette in the soothing cool greens and teals in the design of her dress. He took a deep breath of the soft breeze before wrapping his arms loosely around her waist. When she smiled and leaned back into him, he planted a kiss on her hair, catching a wafting light scent of bergamot and sandalwood.

He wished fleeting moments like these were common. It was his fault. They spent more time together before he took the last job in St. Augustine. When they were married, he would do all he could to be home.

"About your dress, honey, I noticed it," he said softly. "I just forgot to say so. You're right, when we're together, you should have my attention. It's embarrassing that my fiancée is so beautiful and my mind was miles away. I'm sorry."

She half-turned her face back to him with a sad smile. "People say that's how it is when couples marry. The conquest is over and real life dominates us."

With a low groan, Quincy pulled her closer. "Let's pray we're not like those couples. Admit it, we have an outstanding track record of being different."

Mercedes laughed just as the indescribable glow along the horizon lost its brilliance and twilight set in. With his mouth close to her ear, he asked her to go find a bench with him and watch the stars come out.

When they found a perfect seat and settled close together, he draped his arm around her bare shoulders and watched as she used a phone app to see the constellations overhead. They were searching for the right shapes when a shooting star streaked across the velvety darkness.

"Wow!" Mercedes whispered. "Just think, if we were driving, or swimming, or doing anything we do on a typical evening, we might have missed this moment."

Quincy sighed, and his eyes turned thoughtful. "I wonder how much we all miss, every day; chasing work, screens, and entertainment instead of just being quiet, thinking, and relaxing in nature."

With his arm around her, he gave her a quick squeeze. "I don't want to miss the things I should've done, like this or for work. It's tough for me sometimes, you know? It's hard to tell when an opportunity is really for me or if I'm following my own stubborn ambition."

Nodding, Mercedes closed the starry sky app and put her phone away. "Yes, I understand what you mean. Why not tell your dad about it and ask what motivates him to decide on a project? At the very least, he needs to know you're considering taking this on, so he and your mom can pray for you."

"Hmmm. Yeah, you're right," he said, watching a couple board their yacht for the night after having dinner. "He might find the backstory interesting. The evidence I have is from the past, but my team and I are also working with a private investigator and an independent journalist to connect the mystery with someone important in town. This isn't without an element of danger."

He felt Mercedes studying his face, so he turned to meet her eyes. She wore no smile when she said, "Because there's an organization lurking in the shadows?"

Quincy groaned and looked up at the stars. Then he chuckled and raked his free hand through his dark chocolate hair.

Mercedes grinned and pushed her elbow into his ribs. "Are you laughing at me?"

"No!" he blurted, but then he laughed. "No, honey, I'm not laughing at you. I'm marveling at your insight. You don't even realize what you said."

He took her chin with a gentle finger and guided her to meet his eyes. "You asked me if there's an organization lurking in the shadows, and you've never heard of *La Cofradia de la Sombra*."

Mercedes blinked, and he watched her expression as she sorted out a Spanish translation. Wide-eyed, she almost whispered. "The Brotherhood of Shadows?"

Quincy had her attention now, so he dropped his fingertip from her chin. He nodded, letting her make all the connections that were firing in her mind. He loved seeing her like this.

And at that moment, he knew beyond any doubt that his fiancée was the key to his success if he wanted to solve the mystery in St. Augustine, Florida.

Quincy leaned back into the red rocking chair by the harbor, wondering where to begin to tell Mercedes that he craved searching for the truth behind clues found by a Catholic archivist. His mind replayed the conversation he had with Father Sebastián de Morales.

He felt Mercedes studying his face and realized he was biting his lip in concentration. "I got a call one day in St. Augustine, on the dig site. It was an international number, and I almost didn't pick it up. You know what it's like, working when it's so hot you wonder why the heat doesn't melt the sand to glass, and it rises, creating mirages. I looked for a towel and wiped off the coquina dust to pick up the phone."

"Oh, yes, I remember days working like that," Mercedes said. "And I can imagine the scene—you'd answer the call, saying, *Holmwood,* then wait for some thick accent to respond."

Quincy nodded. "Right. Well, your face wasn't on the caller icon, so I didn't say, *Hi beautiful*!"

"Well, I get preferential treatment," she said, tossing her head and running her fingers through her hair.

"Yes, you do. Anyway, a man identified himself as Father Sebastián Morales, and he addressed me as Señor Holmwood."

Mercedes frowned and spoke with mock sincerity. "I'm never calling you that. Did he have the thick accent I predicted?"

Quincy laughed, closed his eyes, and leaned his head back on the rocking chair. Being with Mercedes always eased away the stress he wound himself into. Why had he hesitated to tell her all about this?

He feigned impatience. "Will you just let me get through this story? Yes, the man spoke with an Andalusian Spanish accent, but with a good understanding of English. I only had to ask him to clarify a statement twice. He's an archivist from a diocese in Spain, wrapping up his assignment in St. Augustine. My work with religious relics around the world impressed him, he said. Then he told me my reputation for finding truth and presenting it without the confines of traditional interpretations also impressed him."

Quincy paused, knitting his brows. "Father Morales had my attention now, as you can guess. But it got more interesting when he said I'm young enough to be open-minded at a time when unusual things close minds. He places a high value on the fact that I'm known in the field for honesty and for recovering what others prefer to forget."

Mercedes blew out a long breath of admiration. "Wow, people in the research field don't give out compliments like that every day."

"Right," said Quincy. "I told him that sounded like a blessing and a warning."

"Well said," agreed Mercedes. "What did he say?"

Quincy imitated Father Morales' accent. "It is both, my son. While restoring our archives, I discovered unusual annotations in a seventeenth-century inventory. The handwriting is that of Friar Mateo de la Cruz, a Franciscan friar."

He looked at Mercedes to see what effect his portrayal of the archivist was having on her. She smiled at his acting but tapped his arm as a reprimand. "And? Don't keep me in suspense!"

"Well, now things turned more serious," Quincy said. "I was under the tent for shade and misty air from the fan, but that's not what sent a chill through me. Morales said the friar spoke of a 'confession of blood and coin,' and of a theft committed against the Crown. He also mentioned a secret society. The documents point to something Friar Mateo de la Cruz hid because he couldn't deliver it to the King of Spain."

Stunned, Mercedes watched his eyes, then whispered. "Quincy, do you believe these are authentic?"

"Father Morales assured me they are, and he's a guy who seldom makes jokes. He believes I'm the only one who should see these records before they vanish in locked files again. It sounds cryptic, I know, but he claims there are others in the city who would not want this information to be revealed. We planned to meet at twilight, alone."

Mercedes' brows shot up in alarm, and he held up his hand to still her. "I know that's against my own rules. It didn't help that Morales told me to pray before I came. He said, 'The shadows in this city are not only history.' So, Alex went with me as far as Charlotte Street. He waited in a spot with plenty of people milling around, keeping his phone out as if texting, but using it as a camera to follow me. I was in his sight."

Disbelief was on his fiancée's face. Then she smiled. "You're teasing me, right? There was no clandestine meeting."

Quincy blew out a breath and shook his head. "I wish I were teasing. My impression of Father Morales was that he looked like a nerdy professor, not a priest. He's tall and lean with salt-and-pepper hair. The first time I saw him was eerie, Mercedes. He was shadowy, backlit by the fading light of the day filtered through the Spanish moss. He seemed austere, looking off into the distance, like a scene from a spooky movie. But he heard my footsteps and recognized me instantly."

Wide-eyed, Mercedes said, "Did you feel nervous?"

"Only at the sense of unreality, of another time or something. Not about him," said Quincy. "We shook hands, then he motioned me to a nearby concrete bench. Morales opened a black leather case he had tucked up under his arm. He had photocopies and scans of the relevant portions of fragile documents protected in the church vault. Many had been found behind a false wall panel in a recent renovation where the archives are stored, sealed in a clay jar. Others were found randomly. He linked them to the same friar because of the initials that appear in a church ledger from 1688, and the same initials are carved into pottery from that period. The Friar Mateo de la Cruz usually signed with a capital M de la C."

"But you're a Protestant, Quincy, and worse, you're Baptist," said Mercedes. "Catholics avoid Baptists. Why would Father Morales trust you with this information?"

"I know, I know," said Quincy, nodding and gesturing with his palm up. "I asked why, and he was firm. He said that I'm *supposed* to have it. The information was in an inventory of historic records to be locked away, irrelevant unless he investigates. Father Morales claims it's time for the mystery to be revealed. Sounds ominous, doesn't it? He talks like you."

She burst out laughing and tapped his arm. "I suppose he sounds as if his conviction came from a higher authority."

"Or from something in his family's past, or someone who sent him from Spain. He said he had a personal reason to know if the friar's notes pertain to anything that exists today. But he didn't share it with me," Quincy said.

"True. Father Morales seems to be on a mission to use the information while he can," Mercedes mused. "What was your impression of the records?"

Quincy stared off into the winking reflections of lights on the water, thinking. "Well, there's a fragment of a man's confession, written by the friar, and you know I like personal things. It looked authentic. There was an odd drawing of an hourglass made with black wrought iron with black sand in it, colonial Spanish in style."

He turned to look at her, his eyes serious. "A little serpent encircled the waist of the glass, you know, the narrow part that lets the sand flow down. We guessed the serpent is gold, silver, or brass because the drawing didn't shade it in. It looked medieval—spooky."

Mercedes watched his face, catching his mood. "Is the hourglass in the archives?"

"No. Father Morales said it's the symbol of the Brotherhood of Shadow, a society formed when St. Augustine was being settled. The members were nobles using Catholic trappings as camouflage, meeting in chapels at odd hours and using desecrations of religious imagery in codes. They corrupted town council members, local merchants, and even some soldiers to control trade and divert royal funds."

"That sounds like a mafia, Quincy. What in the world are you getting into?"

Quincy blew out an exaggerated sigh, shrugged, and shook his head. "I honestly don't know, honey. Church records say the friar who left the cryptic notes was murdered, and Father Morales believes the motive was evidence that condemned the Brotherhood."

"Oh, Quincy. You want to be part of solving this mystery. Who else knows?"

"Only you, Alex, and Sonja. They don't have everything I shared with you, but I will reveal it if we find anything that leads us forward."

Chapter 2

The next morning, Quincy called his father to say he would be busy in St. Augustine for the next week. Then he called his trainee, Alex, to confirm his plans.

"Quincy, you're the boss, but I don't understand why you're bringing your fiancée down here," Alex said. "How are you going to keep up with her?"

"She's already made the arrangements. You're staying with me in a condo beside the one Sonja and Mercedes will be in, and those are somewhere on A1A," Quincy answered.

Alex sputtered. "That's out on the beach, not in town!"

"Yep," Quincy quipped in his best imitation of a Southern accent. Most people still noticed he had a slight British accent, so he had been using more words he heard in the Lowcountry. "About fifteen minutes away. Mercedes likes the beach and doesn't know yet that it's safer for her to be out of town. Sounds like you didn't know that, either."

While Alex huffed in indignation, Quincy reconsidered his statement about Mercedes. "Then again," he said, "I'm uncertain about that—she may suspect that it's safer to be out of town and she's getting me away from danger, too. With Mercedes, it's hard to know."

Alex grunted. "What are you saying, boss?"

Quincy laughed and teased Alex about his sensitive spot, which was Sonja, another apprentice. She was cute in a nerdy way and smart, and she wanted Alex to notice both things. The competitive tension between them was stronger than the attraction Alex fought against.

"You haven't done your homework about our new team member, Alex. But I'm sure Sonja has. She will know that Mercedes has a lot of discernment and doesn't overthink things."

The comparison to Sonja hit Alex's ego, and he snorted. "Okay, great, maybe she'll lead us right to our first artifact. And I hope she's good at breaking codes and riddles written in Latin and Renaissance-era Spanish. Because our girl Sonja isn't good at either of those things!"

Quincy's grin faded. "I'm the one who got drawn into this mystery, Alex. Mercedes feels she owes me for helping her handle strange situations with her clients this summer. She's a big-picture thinker, and you and I sometimes focus too much on details. If solving this was easy, it wouldn't remain for us to set right after over 300 years."

Alex sighed. "Yeah, I get it, and I'm with you. Send me the info about the condos and the time you'll get here. Sonja and I will be ready."

"What are your accommodations?" asked Josette, Mercedes' mother, when she called to let her parents know she would be traveling.

Mercedes could not suppress a smile. "I have a roommate and her name is Sonja, so my reputation is safe, Mama. Quincy's roommate is Alex, and both were interns on his last job. Alex admires Quincy and sees him as a mentor, perhaps because Quincy was the youngest archaeologist on that dig. Sonja is very smart, and I'm not sure yet if she and Alex are rivals in their careers or just falling for each other."

Her mother laughed. "Oh, my, well, maybe Sonja needs a good listener? We'll need to pray about that. And I'm glad you can be helpful to Quincy, sweetheart. You've had an eventful summer, and he was around when you needed him most. Maybe you can take some photos and videos for his website on this project. I'll be praying for all of you."

"Yes," said Mercedes. "I'll work on information for his website. We need those prayers, too, Mama, for wisdom and safety. If we discover anything from the evidence, it may link to someone living in St. Augustine today. A descendant. Quincy learned that this man has enough clout that there was a struggle among the City Council members to get the permits to search for the artifacts."

"Sounds like he has a family secret, then, and a reason to keep it buried," said Josette. "Quincy's job is a lot like yours."

Mercedes hesitated. "Well, it is like mine in that the unexpected seems to follow us, but I go to a lot of effort to avoid trouble. Quincy is walking right into it. He isn't even sure he wants to be an independent archaeologist, but he feels drawn to solve this mystery. I believe it's because he's meant to do this."

Josette was quiet for a few moments, then she said, "You're right. It sounds that way."

At the concern in her mother's voice, Mercedes felt a wave of homesickness. She missed her mother and her family. Life was so much simpler when she was younger, surrounded by those who loved her and shielded her from danger. Right now, she had no idea where home would be once she married Quincy. "Mama—I love you."

"Oh! I love you too, honey. We miss you so much, but we're proud of how you've thrived in your career over the summer. It's so obvious that Jesus has a plan for you and that you're following him in it. Please keep us updated about how things are going when you get to St. Augustine and call us if we can help."

Mercedes dabbed away a tear from her cheek with the back of her hand, then sniffed. "Yeah, I'll stay in touch. Tell everyone I miss them."

An ocean breeze caressed Mercedes' hair, lifting long blonde strands away from her ears into the sunlight. They shimmered for mere seconds before settling against her cheeks again. The soft colors of the tropical blooms on her linen blouse played up her sea-green eyes, and Quincy admired her from his seat across the table. They were eating dinner at a popular restaurant on Florida's famous highway A1A, sitting on the deck with Alex, Sonja, and a serene view of the Atlantic Ocean.

Bemused, he studied her face as she quietly assessed his team, and he knew what she was thinking. Or he thought he knew. Sometimes, he imagined he could read her, then she did something totally unexpected.

Sonja and Alex liked her immediately, though Alex acted wary about Mercedes' role as the new member of their team. Quincy guessed his young assistant expected her to be a distraction. But her warm, quiet depth of character charmed him. More importantly, she did not compete with him in conversations as Sonja did.

Mercedes glanced across the table and caught him watching her. With her characteristic quick smile, her eyes softened into the look he thought of as his alone.

"Right, Quincy?" Alex asked, and Quincy was jerked back into the moment. It happened just as their meal was being brought to the table, so he waited, giving everyone time to inspect their food.

"Is everything okay?" asked the waitress with a bright smile. She turned her attention to Mercedes. "I made sure they followed my notes to get yours right."

Mercedes looked up, beaming at her. "Oh, thank you! I appreciate your trouble. It looks right."

The rest of Quincy's team agreed on their orders, and Alex asked for more iced tea and lemon slices. Sonja asked for extra napkins and honey butter for her hushpuppies.

As the cheerful waitress left to get their requests, Quincy offered to say a blessing, and he reached across the table to take Mercedes' hand into his own. They all bowed their heads as he thanked Jesus for his faithful provision. He prayed that the nourishment would sustain them as they served him in the coming days. "If it's Your will that a mystery be brought to light with the evidence You placed in our hands, we ask for guidance, protection, and for all the glory to be Yours. Amen."

His team was echoing his amen when Quincy looked up and saw that a couple at another table watched them. Knowing it was uncommon for diners to see people praying over their meals, he smiled with a nod at them before turning to Alex, who was moving his glass closer to the waitress for more tea. "What were you asking me earlier, Alex?" he asked.

His friend squeezed a lemon slice into his glass, shielding it from squirting on Sonja, and he furrowed his brow. "Uh, I forgot."

Sonja dipped a hush puppy into a small condiment cup with honey butter. "You were asking him about what kind of training Mercedes will need in order to help us."

Alex snapped his fingers and swallowed. "Oh, yeah, that's it. Thanks!"

Quincy turned a knowing look toward his fiancée. "I'll share parts of the research with everyone as we need it. Mercedes knows how fieldwork is done."

"Really?" Alex was genuinely surprised. "You've been in the field? Of archaeology, I mean?"

Mercedes tried not to smile as she nodded, dabbed her napkin at her lips, and settled back into her chair. "Yes, probably a dozen. For example, I worked during excavations at Luxor in the area where artifacts were found that indicated royal items had been crafted there."

Alex looked impressed but unconvinced. "Have you worked on a dig with Quincy?"

Quincy and Mercedes smiled at each other. Quincy said, "Her family traveled to join mine sometimes over the years as we grew up. So, she's seen me at my worst—and my best."

"But you chose a different career," Sonja said. "Why not archaeology?"

Mercedes' smile faded. "Well, I couldn't travel for long because of some allergies I have, especially to foods and animals. Foreign dig sites had no accommodation for special diets, and a person can only live on packed staple food for so long. It was clear Quincy was very good at what he did, and

I physically could not live that life. I saw we had no future together, but I wanted to work in historical settings. So, I chose a career as an architectural historian here at home."

Sonja blinked in surprise. She sat back and stared at Mercedes, thinking the news over.

"It turned out for the best," Quincy said. "The world went nuts, shutting everything down and forcing people to comply with a risky agenda I did not agree with. I lost all interest in international travel and did a lot of soul-searching as I researched the truth behind it all. In the end, I had no desire to be an archaeologist. All I wanted was to endure the world's madness with Mercedes. So, I moved to the States and investigated antiquity theft, only to find that she was drawn into it. But we survived, and the Lord brought us together again, and that's how our summer began."

Both interns stared at Mercedes. Sonja's voice squeaked. "You—you were involved in antiquity theft?"

"Oh, no," Mercedes replied. "No, not at all. My boyfriend's boss was."

"What?" Alex turned to Quincy. "She had another boyfriend?"

Quincy exaggerated a weary sigh. "Only because she thought it was over between us. The story of the theft is long, stretching back several generations in Mercedes' family's past. We didn't realize the connection. Someone nearly murdered her, and the story kept unfolding even after the arrests, eventually ending in tragedy a couple of months ago. Mercedes and I were together again by then."

The interns sat watching Quincy and Mercedes, waiting for more. Mercedes picked up her fork and smiled. "If y'all don't mind, I'm going to finish this blackened grouper while it's hot. It's delicious!"

Quincy took her cue and took a bite of a baked potato. After exchanging glances, Alex and Sonja ate the remaining food on their plates.

The team unpacked their suitcases and some groceries at their condos, and Quincy and Mercedes met for a walk on the beach. The sand was warm under her toes, and Mercedes stopped sometimes to gather a few shells into a small mesh bag she carried.

Quincy indulged her love of seashells for a few minutes, then he gently tugged her arm. "Stay near the surf," he said, and she knew he was going to talk about confidential matters. The sound of the water would mask his words from his cellphone.

A breathtaking sunset on the west side reflected a peach and pink sky in the east, where lavender shadows on the glowing pale gold clouds created a seemingly endless pastel view. Mercedes drew a deep breath as if she could capture it all inside herself. "I wish moments like this lasted longer."

Smiling at her wistful tone, Quincy pulled her closer. They left footprints on their way to the water's edge. "Me, too. That's part of the wonder of it all, anywhere in the world."

Mercedes turned, searching his eyes for hidden meaning. He knew her mind. "Yes, Mercedes, I'm honestly glad I gave it all up. I have zero desire to globe-trot, and I don't feel safe anywhere but here."

Still watching his eyes, she teased him. "But it's not even safe here when you're with me."

"That's entirely different," he said. "When you were gone, I loved and missed the excitement that follows you. But being dragged into a filthy foreign prison indefinitely, accused of being a spy, or shot at for being the wrong nationality, or forced to get an injection before I can work in or leave a country—those things are far scarier to me than the spiritual warfare you entangle me in."

Mercedes smiled and wrapped her arms around him, resting her head on his chest. His heart rate jumped at her touch while they stood in the fading twilight with surf swishing and swirling around their feet. She looked up. "This is fleeting and wonderful, too, holding you, but it's only happening here, of all the places in the world."

He looked down into her teasing eyes and chuckled. "That's why I'll always be right here—wherever you are."

After a few moments, Mercedes pulled back and tucked her hair behind her ear to keep the ocean breeze from blowing it across her face. "Were you going to talk to me about something?"

Quincy reached for her hand and started strolling in the surf. Lacy foam tendrils teased their toes and tugged them toward the water. "Yeah, I wanted to tell you more about that couple I mentioned, the locals interested in my investigation. Juana Gabriel is an independent journalist, and Marco is a detective with the police. They heard about my application to the city council for permission to work on it, and they're curious about what I might find."

They walked along slowly, each in their own thoughts. Mercedes said, "You suspect that they're looking for connections with the secret group you told me about."

Quincy nodded. "Yeah, I do. They know something they aren't sharing with me yet. Alex and Sonja think Juana and Marco are hoping for evidence to expose it."

"Oh," Mercedes stopped walking and turned to him. "How old are Juana and Marco?"

With a shrug, he said he thought they were in their mid-twenties. Then he knit his brows at her expression. "What's bothering you about their age?"

"It's just that none of us, not your team or Juana and Marcos, are even thirty years old. Many people would call us kids. Yet the information we're hoping to find could have serious—maybe even deadly—consequences."

On a moderately busy street in St. Augustine, two men appeared to meet randomly at a line of customers waiting to eat in a popular restaurant. Neither man registered with the pony-tailed young hostess for a table. Casually shaking hands, they traded opinions about the weather before lowering their voices and switching topics.

Middle-aged real estate developer Rick Varela was well-dressed in resort casual business polo and khakis. His tone was oily as he slithered business into his encounter with Victor Saledo, an up-and-coming city councilman still wearing his dress pants and a white shirt that had lost its crispness in Florida's humidity.

"I believe good will come of the approval of the Catholic archives in the hands of that young archaeologist," Varela said. He stretched out a tanned arm and patted the councilman's back, acknowledging that they shared inside information.

"When nothing comes of it all, the matter will finally be over. That's good for me. And when Holmwood fails, your protests of the approval will give you more status on the council."

Victor Saledo considered this, nodding. Then he asked, "Why would the archaeologist bother with that old fool, Father Morales? He is paying Holmwood crazy money to chase thin air—a ghost. All the evidence he has is mystical mumbo jumbo, and I told the council so."

You're the fool, thought Varela, but his practiced smile betrayed nothing. This dullness to spiritual reality was why the membership Victor Saledo sought in the Brotherhood of Shadows was out of his reach. Holmwood was another matter. Varela knew the archaeologist excelled in situations of mystical mumbo jumbo.

"I have men on surveillance," Varela said. "When I get something you can use to elevate your position on the council, I'll let you know."

He stuck out his hand to shake a hearty goodbye and nodded vaguely when the councilman hesitated. The man wanted promises, he knew, but Varela made none. "We'll talk later."

Making his way down the busy street, Varela whispered, "In darkness, it shines." Then, he started whistling a snappy tune that sounded like a broken pirate ditty.

Chapter 3

Mercedes was returning a hurried text to update her family when Sonja called her from the hallway. "Mercedes, are you ready yet? The guys are here."

"Yes, coming!" Mercedes turned her phone off and left it beside a parrot lamp on the nightstand in her room. Then she grabbed her purse and a notebook before going to join the team.

Quincy brightened at seeing her, and she went to accept his greeting with a hug. "Good morning, beautiful," he murmured near her ear. "Did you leave your phone in your room?"

"Just like you said." Mercedes used a silky tone, touching her nose to his cheek. "I like the old-fashioned way of taking notes, anyway. You did a camera sweep of the condo?"

"Yep." He turned off his phone and laid it on the dark granite kitchen counter, back cover side up. An intricate line drawing of a directional compass in golden ink was etched on the expensive brown leather case. "As far as we have the skills for, no one will be spying on us while we discuss the evidence Father Morales trusted us with," he said.

Alex wore a tan-colored T-shirt with a goofy skeleton on the front. Around the image were the words *Archaeology: Like History but Dirtier*. He and Sonja were discussing a recent discovery in South America they had watched on video the night before, and Sonja noted a point he had missed. This irked Alex, but he complimented her conclusion as they turned off their phones. Then he put out his hand in an offer to take her phone to put on the counter, since he was closest to the kitchen.

"I can do it myself," Sonja said. She stretched past him to place it on the counter before turning away.

Mercedes raised her eyebrows at Sonja's curt response. She saw Alex shrug, roll his eyes, and shake his head before he went toward the door.

Quincy met her eyes with a knowing look and a sigh. "Did you get any breakfast?" Mercedes asked him as she pulled a small cooler out of the refrigerator.

He glanced back on his way to the door. "I had some of that fruit we picked up at the store on the way in. And some of the deli turkey."

Sonja brushed past Alex and tugged open the heavy metal door for herself. Alex narrowed his eyes and said, "And I made some coffee in the coffeemaker, just for Sonja, so the condo would smell like it!"

Sonja froze on the threshold, dismay clear on her face. Quincy assured her that there was no coffee in the condo. "That's not true, Sonja, I didn't let him do that." Then he held the door for Mercedes, and as she passed close, he said, "Sonja hates coffee, and the smell of it. I didn't even let Alex open one of those complimentary packets of coffee as a joke."

Alex chuckled in triumph when Sonja glared at him. They all walked to the next door where Quincy and Alex were staying. Sonja glanced back at Mercedes and said, "I know you don't—can't—drink coffee, either. Honestly, I don't get the obsession some have with it, like it's an idol they won't live without. People plaster their morning social media posts with photos of their statement mugs and designer coffee."

In the courtyard, a sunburned man in a crumpled tee shirt waited for his dog to finish making a mess. Then he started scooping it up while the dog watched. Sonja wrinkled her nose. "Same with pets, especially dogs. Too many people make themselves and their finances slaves to them, and they're indignant if they can't force them on others who are allergic or find them dirty or are frightened of them. No human should call themselves a parent to dogs and cats, you know? Human children grow up and take care of themselves. God put humans in dominion over the animals, and the Bible is clear that they are not the same thing."

Mercedes and Quincy grinned at each other while Alex keyed in the code to open the door. "I like coffee okay if someone serves it," he said. "But I can take it or leave it. I agree about pets, though. They are a huge industry, a money pit of pet products and veterinarians. Don't get me started on my theories about the dark realm putting them in our modern lives as a self-medicating distraction from serving the Lord, from fulfilling the Great Commission, and from financial stability and supporting ministries."

As they walked through the open door, Sonja put her hand on Alex's arm. "Wow, we agree on something! I would seriously love to hear your theories about that. I hear people say they prefer their dogs to humans, but this is not biblical. Jesus died for humans, His imagers, and The Great Commission is about serving and sharing Him with humans."

Surprised, Alex stopped, staring at her with genuine admiration. This made her blue eyes sparkle, and she smiled.

"Later," Quincy said. His tone was stern, and he gave Alex a gentle push forward. "This is a fascinating conversation, but we have a job to do: an archaeology investigation. Let's analyze our evidence and plan a next step."

Smiling secretly at the interaction between the two young team members, Mercedes took an insulated cup from her cooler bag. Some would say Sonja woke up on the wrong side of her bed this morning, but Mercedes sensed the young lady was giving Alex a glimpse at things that were important to her. Maybe she was testing his response because she was ignored at home?

Alex and Sonja walked to a dining room table with a view of the boardwalk and the ocean while Quincy looked for a bottle of spring water in the fridge. Without looking back, he announced that the chair with the best view was reserved for Mercedes.

Everyone settled at the table and looked expectantly at Quincy, who put an unfolded map and a stack of papers in the middle, then said they would begin with prayer. Each could join in before he closed it at the end. They prayed for wisdom and sharpness of mind to follow whatever path Jesus was leading them into, and to be able to make progress toward solving the mystery, even if there was no archaeological evidence remaining after so many years.

Mercedes was encouraged by the spiritual maturity of the young couple's prayers. Hers was that if the friar had prayed for truth to come to light, and if it was time for that prayer to be answered, they would be a part of it. She reached for Quincy's hand as he closed out the prayers, and his strong, callused fingers wrapped around hers. He asked Jesus to protect them from all harm and to help him be the responsible leader that the team needed. Then he dedicated their mission to the Lord's glory, to whatever purpose it would serve.

While the archaeology team looked over the papers Quincy had given them, Alex glanced up at Mercedes to ask if she knew anything about the time they were delving into. "We all just finished an important dig here, so ask us if we forget and use shop talk that leaves you out."

Quincy bit his lips into a line to hide a grin and kept his eyes on a map. Mercedes smiled inwardly but kept her expression serious. Alex meant well, and she was not insulted.

She kept her tone mild and interested as she turned a page and looked it over. "Well, I'm not familiar with all the material yet, but I know that in 1688, the backdrop in a harbor town like St. Augustine is in the Golden Age of Piracy. The Castillo de San Marcos was new, so the Spanish occupied St. Augustine, and their ruler was King Charles II, the last of the Hapsburgs."

Mercedes looked up at Alex as if sharing insider information that he might not have heard. "Charles II was nicknamed *The Bewitched* because of health problems from inbreeding. I also know St. Augustine literally sits on top of history. Whenever anyone digs below one and a half feet, an archaeological study must be done. We hope not to deal with such a delay, and frankly, with our modern tools of GPR and similar technology, we only need to follow clues to a location to use them in. As you well know, archaeology is exploding today with finds that there's no time to go dig up. Here in St. Augustine, human remains are reburied under buildings and streets, with no way to identify them. Sometimes a small marker is placed on the site, like the bones they found a few years ago after hurricane flooding in a wine shop on Charlotte Street."

Alex gawked at her, and Sonja grinned. Mercedes collected her thoughts and said, "It's important that we remember that in that era, many secret societies were being formed for different reasons. Both Catholics—including Jesuits—and Protestants were busy creating masonic-style, esoteric, mystical, occult groups in the fifteenth and sixteenth centuries, the Renaissance era. *Renaissance* is French for rebirth, and the idea behind this cultural movement was that man is the measure of all things, not God. Quite a departure from the past, and behind all those secret groups is a quest for personal gain, whether it is prestige or financial. They often hid behind religious props."

Alex struggled not to look impressed as he challenged her again. "Ah. Okay. All right. Well, if we end up searching for clues among the dead, what's the difference between a graveyard and a cemetery?"

"A graveyard is the property of a church, but a cemetery is separate from one," Mercedes said. "In this area, we're likely to see the words *Memento mori* on headstones, which was popular with monks. It translates to *remember you must die*. Today, that sounds morbid—people don't want to think about death—but frankly, I believe the monks were onto something. More of us should consider where we will spend eternity and stop living as if it's here and now."

Sonja laughed and clapped, patted Alex's arm good-naturedly, then turned to Quincy. "Oh, I like her, boss! That's Alex's favorite question to stump people. So, let's give this project a name! What about the *Memento Mori Project*? I mean, the people involved in this mystery who left clues have all died."

Quincy and Mercedes looked at one another and smiled. He nodded to Sonja. "It's perfect. Okay, if Mercedes is one of us now, let's get started by remembering our team goals."

Alex and Sonja blurted out the first thing together. "Protect our professional reputations!"

"Every job is different," Alex added with his memorized response. "We meet the expectations we contracted for and agreed to."

Sonja said, "We work to expose the historical truth. No hiding, preferential treatment, or cover-up."

Quincy nodded, then he turned a solemn look to his fiancée. "Are you on board with us, Mercedes?"

"Yes," she said. "You're the leader, but Jesus is Lord, and the rulebook is the Bible. Unfortunately, this project may put us in the dreaded position of being the sheriff come to town."

The team laughed, and Quincy's eyes filled with admiration. He reached for her hand and kissed it lightly. "It's good to be working with you again, honey."

Beaming, she blew a soft kiss his way. "And I'm always glad to work for the best."

Alex guffawed, then grinned, watching them. "Amen to that, Mercedes," he said. "Quincy's the best."

Their boss flushed as he gave Mercedes' hand a quick squeeze. Sonja sat back with a satisfied chuckle.

Clearing his throat and releasing his fiancée's hand, Quincy said, "Moving on, note the team strategy I have on the third page. We have a public story unfolding, and it's imperative that our team—not Juana Gabriel—controls it. Mercedes, you're in charge of photography. Settings, stalkers, etc."

"Wait—what?" sputtered Sonja, sitting up straight. "Won't a stalker just hide?"

"They can't control being reflected in store windows and won't know I'm not photographing something else," Mercedes explained. "I'll point my cellphone or camera as if I'm photographing something, but I'll have the selfie function on to catch them behind us."

Sonja mulled this over, nodding, and Quincy said, "Sonja, your job is to steer us into camera-rich environments. We must have proof that we aren't treasure hunters or looters. Keep up with security cameras, timestamps, and continuous cloud file backups. Alex, keep me on track, especially with the technology. GPS, Geo mapping, GPR, everything. Record coordinates, chain of custody on evidence, security. The full report and evidence go to Father Morales and the State Archives, proving our team is not profiting from any discoveries we may find."

Then Quincy pointed out another page of notes. "Here's a sample of the obscure clues, messages, and directions I've gathered from the evidence Father Morales shared with me. I didn't include the obvious ones like crosses and religious symbolism—you'll see those on the documents. Be familiar with them, and connections might fire when they pop into our search."

The team studied the page, and Sonja's brows puckered as she read a line out loud. "*In darkness, it shines*. How quaint! So, what is *it*?"

"We don't know that yet, but the Latin translation is very much to the period," Quincy said. "It may sound like a torn bit of poetry, but there's no question this is genuine."

"And worse, it screams *secret society*," added Mercedes. She rolled her eyes. "This is their signature, and once you know it, it's like a neon sign. I believe we'll find that the friar is pointing us to the Brotherhood. All societies use code to talk about special knowledge bestowed only on them as a privileged class of people."

Quincy blew out an exaggerated breath. "Yep. These groups always use a Gnostic style inversion of Christian truth, straight from the playbook in Eden when Eve was promised the knowledge to be like God."

"If it's okay for me to speculate for Sonja's curiosity," Mercedes said, "I'll unpack the likely codes from the motto she's asking about. *In darkness* may represent secrecy, hidden knowledge, and moral compromise. *It shines* is likely to refer to the ambition of the members. They live by works—their own intellect, influence, and control are the *light* and power, hidden from an unworthy world."

"Wow, I see that now," said Alex, jotting down quick notes. "Dare I ask how you know so much about this?"

Mercedes glanced over at Quincy, who said, "Ask her sometime about what happened at her last job. And she's on target about her theory, according to Father Morales."

He looked down at his own notes. "Morales wrote here that he's convinced the messages left by Friar Mateo de la Cruz in 1688 hint at crimes committed by a local secret society of the time called The Brotherhood of Shadows. That hourglass symbol beside their name pops up often. I believe the friar recorded in his own kind of code, a mix of hints that only a true believer could interpret with the Holy Spirit's leading. If you haven't noticed by now, not much about following the friar's trail will be straightforward."

Mercedes nodded with a thoughtful look. "If your instincts are right about the friar's code, he meant for the clues to be understood by the one the Lord sent to make the discovery. As cryptic as these notes sound to us, I can't help but think this will not be difficult to decipher."

Sonja jotted down notes. "Hmmm. That makes sense. It looks like I need to brush up on Renaissance symbolism. Would the friar's code have been the common use in communications of that time?"

"Yes, but it's likely to be more complicated," Quincy said. "Add in the cloak of Catholic traditions of the day. Your translation apps might help you recognize how things were phrased back then. Nobody talks like that anymore."

Alex tapped his pen lightly on his paper, looking off into the view of the ocean without really seeing it. "I was just thinking—about the darkness mentioned in that motto. That's a common theme in Scripture. God knows what's in the darkness and the light dwells with him. If it's time, he will expose the darkness."

Sonja was excited as she reached out to touch his arm. "Yes! If it's in God's time, we might be part of His plan to reveal a cold case crime hidden for so long." She shivered and put down her notebook to rub her arms. "This is getting real for me."

"It better be real; you signed a contract with the Best Boss." Alex's teasing glance swept from her to Mercedes. Then he looked back at the notes Quincy had given them. "What's this weird symbol about? The friar drew an hourglass with a creepy serpent around the middle."

"And worse, the sand flowing through it is *black*." Sonja added, with a shudder. "Is that to represent the darkness?"

Quincy reached for a paper in his notes and slid it to the middle of the table. "The friar's drawing is from about 1688, but Father Morales said the symbol can be found carved into old places around the city. And Juana, the journalist we're working with, gave me a copy of a modern version on a business card. It's an abstracted image, but once you see it, you can't forget the serpentine line around an hourglass."

As the team leaned in closer, Sonja gasped. "Rick Varela? This is his card?" her voice squeaked. "I told you he's slippery, Quincy! Remember when he showed up on the dig site to look around?"

Alex scooted closer to the table. "Quincy, Varela's behind getting the reluctant councilman to approve the permits Father Morales asked for to hire you. He's in that brotherhood, if it still exists. He must be connected!"

"What does he gain from what Quincy may find?" asked Sonja.

Alex scowled, then shrugged. "Well, if Quincy fails, Father Morales said this all gets buried for good. Convenient?"

"Yeah," Mercedes said slowly. "He may want Quincy's expertise to find something—something valuable or incriminating that he can steal or destroy. Maybe the Brotherhood members have been searching for centuries for the evidence the friar hid. And about that serpent—could it be gold or brass? Something that could shine if a light were on it?"

Quincy pulled another page from his stack of research. "Father Morales believes the serpent is gold, and the Brotherhood uses the hourglass in rituals. In that way, it could shine against the darkness of the black sand, in their motto. He also believes the evidence proves the Brotherhood was stealing from the treasury of King Charles. Death records in the archives from 1688 report that criminals mysteriously murdered the friar, and investigators never solved the crime. Morales seems driven to give Friar Mateo de la Cruz credit for his role and justice for his murder."

Alex whistled under his breath. "I know we're speculating and brainstorming here, but could we be looking for a ledger or a list of Brotherhood members who were guilty? Something legal, irrefutable?"

"Yes, and more," Quincy said, his blue eyes somber, looking at each of them in turn. "We may find stolen treasure belonging to Spain in 1688. I don't know what the state of Florida, the country of Spain, and the Catholic Church will do with that. There are antiquities laws, public or personal property laws, and heaven only knows what else. If we get permission to search on someone's personal property and find anything of historical significance, they might get some compensation when the attorneys are finished in however many years it takes. All we know is that this project is approved through the state and city council permits and we are contracted through the Catholic Church by Father Sebastian Morales."

"Okay—okay," said Alex, brushing his hand over his face. "I don't know the rules about that either. It might keep me up tonight. But I know this: whatever we discover, according to our contract with Father Morales, we get credit for it. As far as our careers go, especially if we find stolen treasure, that alone is priceless. And we get paid a flat fee for the effort, then, when the lawyers are done, we get our percentage, per our contract, right?"

Quincy nodded, and his mouth twisted into a wry smile. "We will be compensated, yes, and you're right about our careers. I'll be thrilled for this team. But frankly, that's not my personal motivation. Just as Father Morales feels driven to find justice for the friar, I feel driven to solve the mystery the friar left us—which amounts to justice."

"*The sheriff come to town*, as Mercedes said," Sonja added. "We're with you on the motivation."

Quincy's team studied Father Morales' evidence for hours. When Sonja's stomach groaned out loud, they closed their notebooks and split up to take a break. Alex remained in the condo guarding the evidence while Quincy walked Sonja and Mercedes next door.

Mercedes set down her cooler and unpacked her empty insulated cup while Quincy and Sonja picked up their phones from the kitchen counter. Quincy's phone chimed with a text from Juana asking them to meet her and Marco for dinner at Sunset Grill. Quincy consulted the ladies and then replied he couldn't leave Father Morales' records unattended in his condo, but they were welcome to bring takeout orders instead.

"So, I'll get to meet Juana and Marco," Mercedes said. "Anything I should know about them?"

Sonja adjusted the strap of her pink overall shorts, then turned a knowing glance to Quincy. "Well, Juana has a nose for an interesting story, and she's fair. She picks up the ones most mainstream reporters miss and has a robust online following. Her weekly column in the local city paper is popular. Her boyfriend, Marco, is quiet, but he misses nothing. He doesn't trust Quincy."

Seeing Mercedes' brows shoot up in surprise, Quincy explained. "He doesn't trust me because the city council holdout for this research gave it his blessing. Juana said Marco observed him in a private conversation with Rick Varela just before the vote. Marco's conducting an unofficial ongoing investigation of Varela, and Juana is like a cat waiting for the right moment to pounce on the city councilman. She's gathered evidence on Varela to prove corruption."

Mercedes stood open-mouthed, staring at them. "Are we the bait this couple hopes to use for their own goals and notoriety?" she sputtered.

Quincy scowled. "Well—I hadn't thought of it so bluntly. I hoped this might be a mutually beneficial agreement. Marco is in law enforcement as a profession, so he can offer us guidance and protection. Juana is well-connected and resourceful. She may be able to get access to places for us."

Nodding slowly, Mercedes studied his face. "Have they agreed to all this?"

Quincy shook his head. "No, I haven't heard their position yet. I'm guessing that will happen when we meet tonight."

Sonja nodded. "I think we need a written agreement about expectations all around. Juana and Marco are professionals, but let's face it, Boss—we don't know these people. Part of our rules is to always protect our reputations, remember?"

Chapter 4

From under a black ball cap, a man with peppery colored hair squinted into small binoculars. Deep lines radiated from the corners of his eyes as he peered through the driver's side window of his old black pickup truck. He had changed parking spaces twice at the corner convenience store to throw off suspicion while he watched a short road that led to several private vacation resorts.

His voice was gravelly as he spoke on his cell phone. "They're not all together, co-ed, as you wanted. The ladies are in one condo, but Holmwood and his assistant are in the next one. Sorry, but I got nothing so far for a photo-op that you can use to damage his reputation."

"Hmmm. Disappointing. Can you get into the parking lot?" asked Rick Varela from the speaker on the phone.

"Can't get in at all without a code. I'm on the highway—A1A—at a convenience store, and I've moved several times, but an employee is getting suspicious. I'm moving on after this update before he calls the cops."

"Okay, okay, it's just day one," said Varela on the phone speaker. "No need to risk trouble by breaking into their rooms yet. Take no action unless all of them are gone, understand? They carry and have permits."

"Yeah, yeah, I did my research," said the man in the truck, sounding irritable. "They hit what they aim at, and you don't pay me enough for trouble."

The deep lines around his eyes crinkled again, and he brought his binoculars up. "Hey—wait. They've got guests. Two of them."

He turned his phone to take a photo as Varela said, "Recognize them?"

By zooming in his camera, the spy caught a couple of photos before the visitors disappeared through the door to Quincy's condo. Then he sent them to Varela's phone. "No. Kinda blurry, but see what you think."

His phone speaker erupted in curses and a vile label for the woman. "I should've known she would try to be in on this story! And the guy's a detective—watch yourself. He doesn't dance to the tune at the precinct."

The man in the black cap scowled, staring at the closed condo door. "They had bags, like takeout from a restaurant. They'll be there a while. Maybe she doesn't have a deal for a story yet."

"Maybe," Rick Varela said with a growl. "But I don't like this. Why is the officer there, too?"

As if Varela could see him, the man in the truck shrugged, knowing Varela was thinking out loud to himself. He felt stiff, so he shifted position in his seat. "Holmwood may sense he needs protection," he suggested. "I'll let you know if anything happens. Curly comes on shift at ten; he'll check in."

As an introvert, Mercedes was uncomfortable in crowded situations. There were six people in the vacation condo's dining room, and she barely knew four of them. She switched to quiet mode.

Marco was in a similar mood. He blended in more than he called attention to himself. His intelligent dark brown eyes missed nothing, and Mercedes wondered if he was disappointed that Quincy had put all the evidence for the *Memento Mori Project* in his bedroom.

Sonja grabbed Alex to help her clear away the takeout boxes and dishes when everyone finished their meals and turned to enjoy the expansive view of the ocean through the dining-room windows. Alex looked annoyed as she dragged him away, and Mercedes grimaced. She knew Alex was happy to help. He just wanted the respect of being asked, not ordered, in the company of others.

Juana seemed easy to talk to, and Mercedes wanted to get to know her for the sake of the project. "Juana, do you live in town?"

The reporter brightened. "Oh, yes, I live in my family's home, which was part of the very beginnings of St. Augustine. We have a more modern house now, rebuilt in the 1980s, because a hurricane and then a fire destroyed most of the original foundation. But the gardens and the old family chapel remain."

"Oh, my!" exclaimed Sonja, clearing away the flatware from the table. "That must give you a great sense of being grounded."

Juana's eyes sparkled. "It really does! I wouldn't be so involved in local history if my ancestors weren't anchored here. My parents had me late in life because they wanted to travel the world before starting a family, so they are elderly now. Daddy has dementia, but not the mean kind, and so far, my mom, the housekeeper, and I can manage him at home. Marco helps sometimes, too. Daddy is a terrific source of stories, but I can't rely on them. Whenever possible, I camp out in the historical society and archives to fact-check things he says and piece them together. I hope to finish a project he started years ago about our family history and St. Augustine."

She smiled at her boyfriend. "Our history includes Marco's family. They have always cared for our home, the garden, and the family chapel."

Marco's eyes softened as he met hers and grinned. "That's not a bygone era."

"Yes, but admit it, you're hanging around because of me, and an old family tradition that a revelation will occur someday," Juana teased.

Marco shrugged. "I'm crazy about you, and the housekeeper is a splendid cook, so yeah, I hang out there a lot."

He turned to Quincy's team. "But Juana's right, there could be nothing to the tradition, or maybe it meant something once. The Alvarez family only talks about it among family members, but I shared it with Juana in case her father says something that gives me a clue if it's still important."

Then Marco shifted in his dining chair, knitting his dark brows. "Speaking of mysteries, Quincy, are you free to share anything about your investigation of the documents Father Sabastian Morales gave you?"

Quincy leaned forward, hands clasped over the reflections playing on the glass-top table. He leveled his gaze to hold Marco's. "I'm hoping we can work together and get our goals in writing. I'm not free to share a lot of the information I have, especially with the public. That means I must get permission about what I can release to Juana. What do you and Juana hope to see come of this project? What do you expect us to find?"

Marco's brows shot up, and he exchanged glances with his girlfriend. She nodded, and he turned to Quincy. "Do you believe in following gut instincts?"

Quincy said, "I call it something else, but yes, I do."

Marco studied Quincy, then cleared his throat. "My gut tells me it's time for the truth to come to light about cold case crimes. I believe someone is using you to solve a mystery so he can steal the evidence and ruin you before you ruin him. I want to be around to see justice."

The morning sun was soft over the view of the rolling sea when the archaeology team finished breakfast and considered which clues would be most fruitful in St. Augustine that day. Unlike a puzzle, there was no picture to guide them about what success looked like with Friar Mateo de la Cruz's mysterious messages.

"*Where gold moves by hand, not by horse, God keeps the names on the narrow way.*" Mercedes held her warm cup of tea and read the message, translated from 17th-century Spanish. "I love this!"

"But how does it help us?" grumbled Alex through a mouthful of his bagel. He scowled at the paper in the middle of the table, featuring a copy of an original document with the friar's scribbled riddle.

Mercedes laughed. "Obviously, the friar was leading us to Treasury Street."

After a blink of surprise, Alex quickly wiped his hands on a napkin and started keying in a search on his laptop. "Treasury Street?"

"Yeah," Mercedes said. "It runs inland from Avenida Menendez and Charlotte Street at the waterfront, originally connecting the port to the Spanish Royal Treasury building. It's unique because it's only six feet wide, supposedly intended to discourage pirates and other thieves on horseback or wagons. Since about 1565, treasure was said to have arrived and departed on Treasury Street."

Alex read from his computer screen. "It says here that six feet wide is typical for streets in Spain in that time period." Then he looked up at Mercedes. "How in the world did you know about it?"

Mercedes sipped her cup of lemon tea, and her white linen blouse moved when she shrugged her shoulders. "Probably Atlas Obscura. I like to look up unusual things about places when I travel. When I was here with my family a while back, I was intrigued by the idea of how soldiers or pirates could barely pass through it with a treasure chest between them. We explored it, and I took a lot of photos so that I could create a painting of it someday. There's a quaint old coquina wall there, still intact, original to the settlement years. It just seems to fit the clue the friar wrote."

Quincy was searching for the street on the map of St. Augustine he had spread on the sofa table. "I don't see it. Can you show me?"

Nodding, Mercedes set down her cup and went to stand beside him. She took a tourist map out of her pocket. "Right here," she pointed. "It's more like an alley; no traffic, so look for streets around it. Only the first section is still like the old days, because they've widened the parts near Cordova. If the friar left anything there, it could be in the narrow part."

Alex shook his head. "No way this clue is that easy. We're missing something."

"I can't believe it either," muttered Quincy, following his finger along the map. Then he grabbed Mercedes for an exuberant hug before releasing her to study the map again. "But it's a fantastic first step! Where else would we start, Alex? Find the archaeological surveys about this area and see if there's been an investigation there before. Are there any restrictions in place? Sonja, Mercedes—pack up the gear for a day of hunting down clues."

Rick Varela saw the number on an incoming call and excused himself from a conversation at the office. Stepping outside into the steamy heat of the late morning, he answered abruptly. "You got eyes on Holmwood?"

"Yeah, I followed as they left this morning. Right now, they're looking around the old part of Treasury Street, near the river."

Varela's heart jumped, and he wiped sweat from his brow. Treasury Street? It had never occurred to him. He tried to conjure up an image in his mind, desperately seeking an explanation for Holmwood's interest.

"The old section?" he asked, but he knew the answer. Nothing was left to discover in the modern section of the street.

The man he hired to follow Holmwood sounded impatient. "Yeah, that's what I said. They look interested in that ugly old wall. It's an eyesore, if you ask me. Someone should tear it down."

Varela's eyes widened as he recalled the view of the street. The coquina wall! Was it old enough to play a part in a story he heard from his father about the early days of the Brotherhood? "If it looks like they are damaging any property, send me photos."

"Are you kidding me? They have permission to damage things," the man reminded him with a growl.

"What planet are you living on? Don't you know photos can be useful out of context on the news and social media?" snapped Varela, and he stuffed his phone back into his pocket. Under his breath, he called the spy a foul name.

Mercedes raked back her long blonde hair, laughed, and pulled Sonja to her side, posing for a picture together. "A guy in a black baseball cap is following. Now we have a photo of him behind us."

Sonja played it up, making a heart with her hands for the camera to give Mercedes more time for photos. Tourists in sunglasses strolled by, smelling of coconut sunscreen, checking guide maps, discussing shopping options and seeing most of St. Augustine through their phone cameras.

The archaeology team slowly made their way through the crowds over the griddle-hot sections of the sidewalk, trying to remain as close together as they could. Once they found and turned right onto Treasury Street, Mercedes longed to explore the coquina wall with Quincy and Alex. She and Sonja touched the aging shells and limestone mixture with the men for a few minutes, examining the texture and considering the possibility of the friar hiding anything in it.

But Mercedes knew her role on the team was to watch the man watching them. Sonja slipped into her role, as well, noting any security cameras as she sipped water from a bottle tucked into a mesh pocket on her khaki backpack.

The late summer sunshine washed its warmth over the rough wall, glinting on bits of shell and casting strong shadows. Mercedes' loose white linen blouse was damp with sweat over a white linen tank top, but it was too soon to remove it. She adjusted her sunglasses against the glare, then the lanyard around her neck for her credentials.

She knew Quincy's mind well from his demeanor. It warmed her heart and made her smile to watch his professionalism keep his excitement in check. Unaware that she was observing him, he was like the stereotypical focused archaeologist with high expectations. He lifted his Panama hat to smooth his damp hair back, motioning for the team to gather near him.

Then he took out his cellphone and opened files as he spoke. "Seeing this wall reminded me of a note Friar Mateo made on a document." He scrolled through some photos and stopped. "It may be unrelated, but here it is. *Seek the wall that drinks the rain and shelters words for the King.*"

Mercedes caught her breath and exclaimed. "Coquina drinks rain! It's porous and weakly bonded together."

"*Words for the King*?" asked Sonja, adjusting her jet-black ponytail through the hole in the back of her khaki baseball cap. "Meaning, King Charles, or like, the Lord in heaven?"

Alex rubbed his chin thoughtfully. "The friar was loyal to both. I've gotta admit, I never would've put those two clues together, about the narrow way and the wall that drinks rain."

"They only make sense together when you see this street," said Mercedes. "Quincy is right, the porous wall is here on the narrow way!"

Quincy tucked his phone into a pocket in his cargo shorts. The sunlight beating on his hat brim cast a deep shadow over his blue eyes, but the team caught a gleam of excitement in them. "It's here. Let's find it."

Alex grinned at Sonja and reached for his backpack. "Did you hear that, Sonja? He sounded like my hero! Hey boss, want me to scan the wall for inconsistencies?"

Distracted by his own focus on the wall, Quincy turned when Alex called him and then helped him unpack. Sonja reached into a deep pocket of her khaki overall shorts for a field notebook and pen. Mercedes pretended to be pointing her camera at Quincy and Alex, but she watched the view behind her for the man who followed them. He lifted his head, alerted by their excitement, and took several steps closer. She snapped a clearer picture of his face.

"We're being watched, and a few tourists are curious," she reminded the team in a low voice. "We might end up on social media."

Keeping his eyes on the equipment he and Alex were setting up, Quincy said, "Surprise him, honey. Turn around and take his picture full on."

Brightening, Mercedes spun around and took two photos of the watcher before he could react. She waved and called, "Want to join us?"

The disoriented man took a few steps backward, then he recovered and started a brisk walk to the main road, disappearing around the corner while tourists snickered. Sonja doubled over in laughter, and Alex guffawed. Quincy glanced at his fiancée, winked, and grinned. "Zeke would be proud of you. I'm going to text him my version of what you just did."

Mercedes shrugged, and Sonja asked who Zeke was. Mercedes said he was her socially graceful, outgoing older brother. "He likes to tease me out of my inhibitions," she said as she examined the photos. "Hey, Quincy, I got a clear view of the guy's face. Shall I send these to you? Do Juana and Marco need to help us identify him?"

Quincy stepped over to take a look. "Yeah, these are good. I'll get them to Marco. He can track whether this man is known to be dangerous." He started a text with Marco.

"Hey!" Alex yelped. "I got a reading on something. It's right here. A narrow cavity, but something else is in it."

Quincy quickly hit the send button on his phone and handed it to Mercedes. Then he was by his assistant's side, squinting at the image on the non-invasive GPR scan where it pointed at a spot on the old wall.

Mercedes wanted to go closer, but her role was to be on alert for spies, and maybe Quincy's phone secretary, since he left his with her for Marco's response. She glanced around. The man in the black baseball cap had not returned.

Sonja touched her arm. "He's gone. Let's record the search on the wall for a report. I'm jotting the notes. You get the video."

For the recording, Quincy was all business, and he unconsciously slipped back into a more noticeable British accent. "Looks like we have a narrow, air-filled cavity, roughly an inch and a half wide." He raised the handheld radar again, sweeping the sensor over the wall's surface. "It's only about an inch from the surface now. I'm getting visual confirmation without damaging the wall."

Anticipating what Quincy would need, like a nurse assisting a surgeon, Alex handed him a thin masonry bit. Quincy pressed it into the mortar, and the whine of the drill softly pushed powder onto his gloved hand. Then he pressed his borescope into the pilot hole made by the bit. His camera probe was no wider than a pencil eraser, and on Alex's screen, darkness gave way to a rough shell texture, then a glint of glass.

"Wait!" Alex breathed, tense. "Look at this."

He held the screen so Quincy could see the green curve of colonial glass, crusted slightly with salt bloom. Through the glass, the bottle seemed to contain something fibrous.

Quincy turned to the ladies. "Sonja, call Father Morales. Use my phone. Tell him it's important that he get here right away."

Mercedes handed Sonja Quincy's phone and continued the video she was recording. Quincy resumed his report. "We've found a small glass bottle, maybe five inches long and about an inch wide. It is intact and contains something pale and fibrous."

Quincy set the borescope aside and unrolled a bundle of conservation tools. Mercedes tried to remain calm about the discovery and focus on the process as she ran her video camera over the soft brushes, bamboo picks, and a low-pressure micro-suction tube with a nylon tip. Viewers were always curious about the tools he used. She focused on Quincy again as he said, "I'm attempting to clear it."

Inserting a bamboo pick into the pilot hole, the young archaeologist broke away loose mortar dust around the bottle's shoulder. Shell grit dislodged inside the cavity, and Quincy followed with a micro-suction tool which drew out the powder.

"The bottle is free. It was never in the cavity tightly," he said. "Now I'll ease the bottle out."

Alex knew what Quincy would ask for and had it ready. "Come on," he coaxed the artifact under his breath. "You've been waiting in there for over three hundred years. It's time to tell your story."

Quincy was silent, focused, using delicate pressure to ease the small bottle forward. When it came out, he stared at the greenish glass with the amber seal around it. Then he held it up, speaking to the camera again.

"This bottle is perfectly preserved, and the contents are sealed in beeswax. Inside is a tightly rolled message. Now we put it in a padded conservation box for the lab, where it will be opened in a controlled environment. If it's intact and we can unroll it, we'll release the information to the public."

A tourist blurted, "But you have an idea about what it is, right?"

"Yes, sir. If it's what I'm looking for, it will lead my team to something else, and maybe something more. Archaeology is often like that. Be watching the news to hear about what we've found and how it represents life in St. Augustine in the time it was hidden here."

"So, you believe it was put in the wall to keep it a secret," said another tourist.

"I see no other explanation for why it would have been put there and covered, do you?" Quincy asked with his characteristic charming grin. "But things that are hidden eventually come to light. Maybe that's our life lesson for today."

"Let's go see what the friar wanted the king to know," whispered Mercedes.

Treasury Street, St. Augustine, FL
By Pamela Poole

Marco Alvarez rushed to Treasury Street after getting a text from Quincy. He arrived to see a small band of tourists gathered around the young archaeologist, who was holding a glass bottle in a padded box. The sun reflected off the item with a flash that made Marco blink.

He almost reached for his weapon when another man hurried up to the team, but he quickly recognized the visitor in town. Father Sabastian Morales was the intriguing Spanish archivist who hired Holmwood. He must have been summoned, and he came quickly, just as Marco had.

The investigator relaxed a bit, but he scanned the area for the man in the photos Quincy sent, reporting he had been following them. There were a few scattered heads with black baseball caps on them, but none were the man in the photos.

Holmwood looked up, met his eyes, and nodded to acknowledge him. He thanked the tourists for their interest and introduced Father Morales as the one in charge of getting any discoveries to local conservation labs and the proper chain of custody.

"My team and I are not treasure hunters, like in romantic adventure novels," Quincy said with his charming grin, and Marco almost laughed. The archaeologist was using this free publicity to get ahead of the accusations that were surely part of Varela's plan to discredit him. The more Marco learned about Holmwood, the more he trusted him. He was beginning to see what Father Morales saw—Holmwood was smart, experienced, and grounded, and he spoke with confidence and authority beyond his years.

But there was something else about Holmwood that set him apart, something hard for Marco to put his finger on. Something—righteous.

Quincy wrapped up his interaction with the tourists by inviting them to visit his website. "We've been hired for a job here that may lead to an exciting revelation about the past—or it may lead nowhere. That's the reality of this profession. Remember that if your children want to become archaeologists."

The local conservation lab was familiar to Quincy from past work in St. Augustine. It smelled faintly of ethanol wipes, clean cotton, and the metallic dryness of filtered air. The sealed vial he had pulled from the old coquina wall on Treasury Street now sat on a padded tray inside a glass-walled humidity chamber while a technician checked the digital readout. It was safe to open the seal and draw out the paper and parchment.

The technician recognized him. She smiled, knowing he could do this as well as she could. Then she slipped her hands into the built-in glove ports while Quincy and Father Morales watched. Selecting a scalpel and padded micro-forceps, she slid the blade under the edge of the wax. A thin shard of it lifted away, then another, until the cork was exposed. She exchanged the scalpel for the forceps and gripped the cork's top edge, rocking it gently to avoid internal suction.

Father Morales clasped his hands and clenched them. It was the first sign Quincy had seen that the somber Morales was excited, and he felt better about his own anticipation. He maintained a professional demeanor because he dared not assume yet that he had found a letter well over three hundred years old, written by a Franciscan friar to King Charles II about crimes committed against the crown. Could Mercedes be right in saying that finding it was a calling for such a time?

He wished his fiancée and his team could be here to share this moment, but access to the labs was restricted. They were working in the cramped lobby, compiling notes about the discovery as they waited for him.

The cork yielded with a soft *pop* inside the chamber. Father Morales exhaled a long breath, and the technician glanced at him, then smiled before setting the cork aside and angling the bottle to grasp the rolled paper. Inserting a slender wooden lifter, she coaxed the roll toward the opening, and it slid with ease before dropping gently into her waiting palm.

Father Morales' eyes were locked on the fiber roll as he asked, "What happens now?"

The technician set it on a sheet of acid-free paper inside the chamber. "We'll acclimate it for about three days, then unroll it, millimeter by millimeter." She looked up into his eyes, then at Quincy. "If this is what you think it is, we'll listen to a man who left a message for us a long time ago."

Chapter 5

Father Morales invited Quincy's team and Marco to dinner with him in the private dining room of a quiet restaurant nearby, assuring them their working attire was acceptable in his arrangements. It was an occasion to celebrate, yet he was too alert, looking up and lowering his voice every time the door opened. This set Mercedes on edge.

As she finished her raspberry sorbet, Morales announced he was arranging extra security for the team and that guards were already stationed at the conservation lab. "Marco informed me about the police record of the man who followed you today," he said gravely. "There is never conclusive proof that he has caused—accidents—but he is always on the scene, and there's no question about his connection to Rick Varela, a local real estate developer who is notorious for shady business deals."

He waved his hand as if to ward off their protests and said, "I know what you found is unrelated to his properties. The item found in the coquina wall predates his lifetime. However, the Varela family has very old ties in St. Augustine, and our discoveries might affect his reputation."

Mercedes' eyes widened as she searched her host's face, finding concern all over it and trying to read what he was not saying. A sudden shiver ran up her spine that was not caused by the frozen sorbet.

She briskly rubbed her arm with her hand. There was an element of danger the team acknowledged from the beginning, but the threat on the first day in the field surprised her. Though she was grateful for Father Morales' protection, what would this mean for the team? Was Quincy the main target now?

Mercedes turned to him and found a scowl on his handsome, tired face. "Is there danger for us at our resort?" he asked Morales. "We have no artifacts, nothing of value to a man like Varela."

Father Morales nodded and turned to Marco, who cleared his throat and leaned closer to the long table. "The condos are easy to guard, but you need to split up on the drive there and back. We believe Varela hoped you would find treasure as irresistible as he does and go for that first. I doubt he expected you to find a tiny bottle of colonial-era glass with a message in it, and he may try to get his hands on that information before you can. If he can stop you or slow you down, it will be to his advantage."

"Let's be honest," said Father Morales. "It is shocking to a man like Varela that on your first day out, your team made a major discovery. I'm the only person who expected this." He smiled and pointed at Quincy and Alex. "Admit it, you did not. I believe the friar intended for the right person to decipher the code to his clues with the guidance of the Holy Spirit. Varela can't fathom this."

Quincy looked at Father Morales for a moment, then at Mercedes. "You're right, Father, neither Alex nor I expected what happened today. But you were not the only one who did. Mercedes told us yesterday that she believed the clues would be understood as we came upon them."

Alex squirmed in his seat. Mercedes smiled shyly and felt a surge of confidence. She reached for Quincy's hand under the table and made sure he read calm confidence in her eyes.

It worked. The tension on Quincy's shoulders relaxed. He sighed deeply, rubbing his thumb over the back of Mercedes' hand. "What's the alternative for our stay in the vacation rentals?" he asked, looking from Marco to Father Morales. "Does staying in St. Augustine give people who mean us harm easier access?"

Marco nodded. "Yes, it does. There's no safe alternative, Quincy, I'll be upfront about it. You brilliantly stomped out any chance for the signature tactic that Juana and I expected Varela to use first, which was to discredit you as a treasure hunter. He has no social media accounts in his name, just fake ones we tracked to his computer. While he can make trouble for you and cast doubt on your reputation, he can prove nothing. This could make him desperate."

"Does he have any idea what's in that bottle we found today?" Alex asked.

Father Morales spoke now in his thick, but understandable, accent. "I risk sounding as cryptic as the clues the good friar left for us, but I think Varela was surprised by the location and nature of the artifact. His best guess as to the contents would be a treasure map or a list of names, and he needs both. His ancestor's names are on that list, and he will not want them to be known. But it's not silver and gold, which is his language, and he must find it. Trust me, Varela is very nervous tonight."

In a shadowy corner of a small cafe, Rick Varela drummed his fingers on the polished tabletop. His dark eyes kept darting to the door. He was early, but what else could he do? Concentration on business was impossible today.

A man appeared at the door and walked in, calm and purposeful as he scanned the dining room. Varela tried to hide his relief. The man he was meeting made his way to the table and sat down. Then a waitress came to the table to take their orders. Both men looked nonchalant as they studied the menu and ordered sandwiches.

Curly worked for Varela, sometimes doing temporary scouting jobs. He blended well into the crowd. It was unclear where he got his nickname because he was bald and owned a variety of baseball caps, Panama hats, and beanies. Varela knew he was not Curly's only employer, which meant others trusted him, too. Since Curly never tried to act chummy with Varela, he could only count on the scout's reputation, not his loyalty.

"I heard about the way the archaeologist's team got rid of your photographer today," said Curly, lazily reaching for the warm chips and dip in the middle of the table. "Guess he's no longer working on this assignment."

"Never mind him, it's worse than that," Varela growled. There was no need for Curly to know he had other arrangements with his first scout. "I need to know what's in that old bottle Holmwood found. Morales has that lab covered with security like Fort Knox."

Curly shrugged and crunched another chip. After swallowing it and a sip of his iced tea, he said, "I thought you wanted that archaeologist to discover a valuable artifact that you would quickly relieve him of, leaving him to take the blame for its disappearance."

Was his plan so transparent? "The bottle was not part of the plan," Varela said without confirming or denying Curly's guess. He tried not to grind his teeth.

The men fell silent as the server brought their meal. When she refilled their iced tea and left the table, Varela said, "It could contain information I don't want in public."

Curly's hand froze with his fresh sandwich halfway to his mouth. He studied Varela's small black eyes and set the sandwich down. "Such as?"

Varela shook his head and swallowed the bite he was chewing. "Don't look so suspicious; it might be nothing. But it could be the location of something I've been looking for a long time."

Varela suddenly put down his sandwich and leaned forward, hoping the desperation he felt was not on his face. Curly still looked wary, and there was no good reason to spook him. Varela smiled and spread his hands. "Look, just keep me informed about where they are, and I may figure out why. I could find what I'm looking for. There's a huge bonus in it for you."

Curly looked thoughtful as he turned his attention to his sandwich. They ate without more conversation until the waitress came to take their plates and Varela paid the check. Then Curly looked across the table and asked what his orders were.

Varela shifted in his seat. "Holmwood's team is only working daylight hours, but I have no idea where they will be. They have eyes on anyone following and all security cameras. I believe that Detective Marco Alvarez has them on alert, and it will be hard to watch them. You're my best. Can you do it? Do you have anyone else who can help?"

"You only want eyes on them, photos, and an instant alert of any discoveries, right?" asked Curly. "I can get help if that young lady nails me, but he costs the same as me, and neither of us causes bodily harm, accidents, or commits crimes."

Varela nodded and suppressed his eagerness. He shook hands with Curly and said, "Surveillance is the job, and you can assure your friend, if we need him, that I'm good for the money."

As Varela parted with Curly, he wore a smirk. *Don't worry, Curly,* he thought. *Someone else will handle accidents and crimes.*

Marco walked outside the restaurant with Quincy's team after dinner with Father Morales. The plan was to accompany them to their rental truck, then Quincy and Mercedes would ride with him and follow the truck behind Alex and Sonja.

"Don't you get any time off?" asked Alex as they followed the sidewalk past shuttered small businesses. There was little traffic on the street.

"I'm off duty now, but on duty with Father Morales' church payroll," said Marco. "It's been a strange day."

Sonja snorted. "Ya think? *Strange* is one way of putting it. Creepy is my personal description."

Alex grinned and nudged his elbow into her ribs. "But it's like being Indiana Jones, right? Admit it, archaeology is more boring than we expected in school. This is what I got into this field for."

Flickering gas lanterns and the strong glare of streetlights made an eerie path on the roughened sidewalk. Stark, spooky shadows loomed under tree shapes as the group reached the corner where the pickup truck was parked.

"Ah, yes, I know you got into this because Indiana Jones never went to find evidence for the Nephilim," Sonja teased, then she laughed. "The movie wrongly connected elongated skulls with aliens. You're planning to pick up where he failed you. Now you'll get practice running from the powers who keep ancient secrets like that!"

As the couple laughed together about popular archaeologists in movies, Mercedes took a deep breath of the salty scent and distant rain. Quincy was quiet, holding her hand as they followed, and she left him to his thoughts. The white truck came into view. It was parked in a small lot under a sprawling live oak where Spanish moss swayed like ghostly arms, luring the unwary into dark shadows.

Alex jangled the truck keys he was now in charge of and opened the door for Sonja. They continued their lighthearted archaeology banter as she got in without a protest. He waved at the others, saying he would see them at the condo, and went to the driver's side.

"Wait!" Marco said, stopping abruptly and extending his arm. "Do you hear that?"

Alex and Sonja were behind the windows in the truck, but Quincy and Mercedes stood near Marco. They heard the scrape of metal on pavement, and oncoming headlights blinded them.

"Quincy—" gasped Mercedes, instinctively reaching out. A dark sedan rolled toward them, engine off, picking up speed.

It coasted diagonally across the sloping parking lot, straight at them.

Marco exploded into action just as Quincy realized what was happening. He shouted, grabbing Quincy by the arm with one hand and Mercedes' wrist with the other, yanking them away. They stumbled and landed on the pavement as the sedan slammed into a coquina wall, which cracked and crumbled.

Alarms shrieked, but not as loudly as Sonja when she ran to them from the truck. All Mercedes could hear for a few moments was the thunderous echo of the impact between the sedan and the wall. Then, in panic, she looked for Quincy, who lay on the ground.

"Quincy! Are—are you okay?" she stammered, trying to sit up, brushing grit from her palms.

Alex was running towards them, shouting over the clamor of alarms and sirens. "There's no one in that car!"

Marco scrambled up from the rough pavement, saw that Mercedes was unhurt, and rushed to help Quincy. "I'm okay," Quincy said weakly as Marco took his pulse. "I think I just got the wind knocked out of me."

Father Morales heard the alarms and ran to the chaotic scene, scanning it to see if Quincy and his team were involved. Sonja had a tissue, brushing some blood from a scrape on Mercedes' elbow. Alex went to the truck for a first aid kit, and Marco helped Quincy sit up but kept him on the ground.

Quincy stared at the crushed fender inches from where his ribcage might have been if Marco had been a second too late. Remarkably, peace washed over him, and he whispered, "Jesus, I'm here for a reason, and You protected me—us—tonight."

Father Morales crossed himself and murmured under his breath as the significance of what had happened sank in. He and Mercedes went to Quincy to keep him down while Marco called in his report and asked for an ambulance.

"I'm okay, honey," Quincy told Mercedes, patting her hand in assurance. "In fact, I'm better than okay—I'm certain now, certain about what I'm doing here. Someone wants me dead because of what I might find. Whatever Friar Mateo hid so long ago matters. Tomorrow, we'll follow more clues."

Juana sat through the dark early morning hours in the comfortable living room of the resort condo that Sonja and Mercedes occupied. She had seen the two exhausted women to bed. Next door, Marco watched Quincy and Alex in their condo, and outside, two security officers roamed the premises. It remained to be determined whether the team was safer here on Anastasia Island or in town.

She wriggled under a cotton throw blanket deeper into the sofa cushions and mused over her father's stories as she kept watch. The latest of his ramblings unnerved her, especially after Quincy's team discovered a bottle that could contain a message from Friar Mateo de la Cruz. Yesterday, her father said, "The friar in brown robes told me stories when I was little. He was always covered in coquina grit and he said, *Gabriel is guarding what evil men tried to steal.*"

She wrote it down in her notebook of things to research but had no time yet. Half an hour later, as she helped her mother put him to bed, he said, "Your ancestor Alonzo wrote his sins down on paper and buried them because he was scared and ashamed. He hid them to be guarded by the angel and asked God to cover them in darkness until the time came to know."

Her mother squeezed his hand and said, "Darling, Marco is not here right now. Shall we tell him about Alonzo when we see him?" Then, her father looked confused, and she wondered if he thought Juana had married Marco.

But the most startling story came this morning as she had breakfast with her parents before covering a news story. Her father lapsed into one of his spells, and he said, "Men with the snake and hourglass followed our family, keeping the time, always keeping the time." Juana had frozen at this, knowing the symbol spoken of was the emblem of the Brotherhood of Shadows. Quickly, she jotted this down in her notebook to tell Marco.

She used to believe her father's delusions were from dementia. But lately, she saw real-world counterparts in them. Was her father a keeper of a tradition he didn't understand? Did he know instinctively that he was supposed to pass this tradition on to her?

Rick Varela was trying in vain to shout. The effort awakened him, and he bolted upright, throwing back his bedcovers and gulping for air. The darkness in his bedroom was relieved by a light on a phone charging station on his nightstand, and his eyes darted around. A moan of fear escaped his throat, but he was alone.

He swiped a shaky hand across the sweat on his face and took a deep breath. It had been a dream, but worse than any of the recent ones he had had. What was this about? If this were a message, why would the man not speak?

Rick closed his eyes, recalling the dream on the wakeful side. An elderly man, clearly wealthy, stood near him wearing fine but practical clothes of linen and silk made in another era. In one gnarled hand, he held the hourglass of the Brotherhood, with the shining serpent tightening its grip around the middle. The other hand caressed the contents of a very old-style strongbox, like pirates used, and he gently grasped gleaming coins and let them slide into the box again.

The man turned from smiling into the box and looked directly at Rick. The face was familiar, like an old portrait he had seen somewhere, and the skin looked like crumpled parchment that had been smoothed out again. But the eyes terrified Rick. They were black voids with no spark of life, and to peer into them was a slide into infinite darkness.

As Rick reeled under the stare of the merciless eyes, the man—or apparition—lifted his bony hand from the coins and used it to point at him. Rick staggered backwards, asking what this meant, but the awful visage only grinned. Shouting his question in a panic, Rick awakened himself—with no answers.

He rubbed his face with his hands, trying to shake off the dream and get some sleep. There were two deals to be closed in the morning at the office.

Rick Varela left his bed and went to the bathroom, unsettled, trying to escape the cobwebs of a nightmare that clung to him. His mind would not turn off the replay of the ending. What did it mean? Was it a warning, or an assignment?

A sudden memory of his father's headstone made him jerk back up as he settled into bed. The hourglass! How much sand was left in the one in his dream?

Try as he might, he could not conjure up the image of the hourglass on the man's arm. And this shook him to the core.

There was a way to find out. Why had he not done this before Holmwood arrived? He was the only member who remained in the Brotherhood of Shadows. It would take some planning, and he must be extremely careful, but he knew of no other way to get what he wanted without following the Brotherhood's dark instructions in a neglected antique book.

"I've been thinking," said Alex. He half-turned from his laptop when he heard Quincy enter the open living area and move toward the refrigerator. "We know the best conditions to find artifacts in around here, from our last job. But I think there's money involved in this project. Big money. Which means a strongbox."

He sat back in his chair and talked through a mouthful of toast and jam. "Has to be money. We need a team from the conservation lab to extract a loaded strongbox from that era. We can't pick it up."

Quincy winced from reaching for a container of organic fruit juice. "Done," he grunted. "Father Morales made the arrangements. What makes him nervous is whether the extraction team arrives on the scene before the guy who wants that money."

Alex groaned. Marco rose from his chair at the dining table and carried an empty plate to the kitchen. "Sore today?" he asked Quincy.

Quincy nodded, swallowing some juice. "Not too bad, and I slept well. Just stiff. Thanks to you, I'm here to talk about it."

Marco shrugged and put his plate in the dishwasher. "I was looking for trouble; you weren't."

"I am now," Quincy said, reaching for turkey bacon. "Maybe I need to know my enemy better. Got any ideas?"

Marco leaned back against the dark granite kitchen counter, crossing his arms and studying Quincy. "Can you go for a ride with me? Everyone else must stay here and work on the research. I can't watch them all."

Glancing at Alex, who turned in his chair to watch, Quincy said, "I can be away until noon. The guys outside aren't the babysitters?"

The expression on Marco's face did not change. "I'm the last stand here, Juana's the last stand for the ladies."

Quincy kept chewing a bite of the bacon, keeping his eyes locked on Marco. Then he swallowed and smiled. "Well, if it's any comfort, Mercedes and I have your back."

He turned to Alex, who grinned from the dining table. "Alex, start that research on depictions of Gabriel and angel wings around St. Augustine, and the history of who once found these meaningful. Print out all the Bible verses where Gabriel is mentioned and compare our riddles and clues to see if there's a link. I'm getting dressed to go out with Marco for a while to research another angle on all this."

Chapter 6

In the passenger seat of Marco's car, Quincy texted instructions to Mercedes and Sonja about research to be done until he returned. He looked up when Marco parked at an old bank building that had been repurposed as a stationery and gift shop. After looking all around the area for anything suspicious, Marco nodded at Quincy, and they stepped out into the wilting summer heat.

Marco gestured with his head to the front of the building and stopped when they reached a large stone in the foundation. Quincy studied it. "A cornerstone?"

"Yes, among several still intact around the city. But it's not just any cornerstone." Marco squatted and laid a finger on an obscure point at the bottom. "This is what I wanted you to see."

Quincy pulled his Ray-Ban sunglasses to the top of his head and squinted; then he got down beside the investigator. Startled, he glanced at Marco and back at the emblem tattooed into the stone. Then he took out his phone and photographed it, up close and in the context of its place on the cornerstone of the building.

"The man who built this bank was one of Varela's grandfather's mentors and best friends, among the last of the traditional members of the Brotherhood of Shadows," said Marco. "I have a list of names I've been tracing. The group had to change over the centuries, adapting to the times. When more popular secret societies established themselves in the city, the Brotherhood shrank to mostly ancestors, in-laws, and influential friends of the original charter members. Perhaps they feared extinction, so they left their mark on places where they held power."

Quincy nodded while his mind did the math about the centuries and the generations involved. "Rick Varella came out to the last job site I worked on. Not to see me. His business was with the sponsor. Is Varella the last one left of the Brotherhood?"

Marco looked around, checking their surroundings. "Yes. But he has shown signs of interest in recruiting, rather than keeping the money and secrets for himself."

"Anything unusual about how the members died?" Quincy asked, then looked startled. Why had he asked such a question?

Marco grimaced. "There were no senior citizens among them. They all died suddenly, many in strange accidents or suicides."

Staring at Marco, Quincy mulled this over. "Then why—"

"Why become a member?" asked Marco. "Most were raised in it, as a heritage and honor from elite Spanish bloodlines. Others were chosen for the power they brought to the group. There were wealth and other great advantages to belonging to *La Cofradia de La Sombra*—the Brotherhood of Shadows—while you were breathing. These men were wealthy and powerful until the railroad and hotel tycoons came in with their own societies."

Quincy nodded. "How many of these hourglass cornerstones are there?"

"I've found three on public buildings, three more on historical residences that have changed hands," said Marco. "They date to different eras. If you need the photos, I can share mine. There are a couple in public parks, like on concrete or stone seating, a memorial plaque on a tree planted in memory of someone, a few stamped pavers donated around town, with the emblem and motto on them. And there's a library shelf donated in memory of the man who owned this bank."

Quincy's eyebrows shot up. "What kind of books are in that section?"

"I knew you'd ask," said Marco. "All I could find were books on finance, investing, economics, and business."

He turned to lead Quincy back to the car. "I've already fanned through the pages for any notes or material left inside them, but apparently the library itself oversees what is stocked on that shelf. I found no references to the emblem or the society, nor to correspondence being passed through the books secretly."

As he fastened his seat belt, Marco said, "Now you've seen this, I hope I've prepared you for the next stop."

The cemetery was old but well-cared for. The weathered headstones gave it far more personality than the endless rows of flat plates in modern burial sites. Quincy had always enjoyed jaunts through old cemeteries and graveyards because the ghostly epitaphs that were still readable on the headstones revealed so much about the lives people had lived. They had a time to walk the earth, and some left a statement or Bible verse that expressed what they did with that time.

In the American South, people left coins and seashells on many graves, and this cemetery was no different. When Quincy once investigated what this meant in Southern culture, he found the sentiment varied among visitors and loved ones.

Sometimes it connected to the safe passage beliefs pagan cultures had for loved ones who needed money to cross the river Styx, and sometimes visitors paid respect for the military service given by the deceased. Shells, especially scallop shells, seemed to be connected to some old Christian traditions, but the shells were also a sign of respect placed on graves, not out of any afterlife beliefs, but because it was something everyone else did.

Marco led him through a maze of graves, and among the flowers, coins, and seashells, Quincy often saw the motto his team had named their project. *Memento mori,* he thought. *Remember, you must die. What will people remember about me?*

His musing ended when Marco stopped in front of an old family burial area. A low, weathered wall, only a few stones high, set it apart. Spanish moss draped over sprawling oak limbs like old men's beards, shedding bits onto the graves below. This site was to be seen and remembered, not kept in seclusion, and he followed Marco to look over the memorials.

He paused when he saw the newest headstone. "Varela? Rick's father?"

"Yes. He died in a bizarre fire about ten years ago, on a construction site that the company oversaw. His wife had died earlier that year of cancer, and Rick has no siblings." He pointed at the engraved message Varela left for the world. "There's a theme repeated on each male headstone in this family plot. Not always worded the same, and not all ancestors are here. Records say some traveled to other holdings they had, such as plantations. There is a lot of evidence that the Brotherhood was involved in human trafficking."

Quincy squatted before the headstone bearing the name, birth and death dates of the deceased. The tribute to his life claimed only that he was an important figure in the betterment of the historic city. Below this, Quincy saw the hourglass. Blackened etching indicated black sand, and a serpent coiled around the slender waist of the glass. Barely visible in the shade of the oak tree was a tiny date and an inscription under the hourglass.

He steadied himself with one hand on the grass to read a date and an inscription. *1688.* Breathlessly, he muttered the message aloud. "*Time will settle the account.*"

Marco nodded. "Sounds like a threat to me. The motto near the bottom of the stone is in Spanish. It links the deceased to the Brotherhood."

Quincy nodded and mumbled the translation as Marco read it. "*In darkness it shines.*"

Both were silent then, studying the inscriptions on the Varela monument. Then Quincy stood and read it aloud again in the quiet cemetery. "*What the traitor hid will be reclaimed. Until the appointed hour is fulfilled and the silver and names are returned, the Brotherhood does not rest.*" He turned to Marco. "Almost sounds biblical. I'm sure that's by design. Only the members would understand."

Marco nodded. "And it casts the good guy as a traitor. I believe they killed Friar Mateo de la Cruz. This is why I warned you of lurking danger."

Looking back at the inscription, Quincy re-read it aloud. Then he said, "I understand why you warned me. This is in the future tense—*until the appointed hour is fulfilled.*"

"It's not a remembrance for a dead man," Marco said. "It's an assignment of vigilance for the living about something that lies ahead."

"Look at the hourglass," Quincy said, pointing at the symbol. "There is sand left. Time for the fulfillment of the appointed hour."

"Want to see something creepy?" Marco asked on his way to an older headstone. "There's more sand in this one. And more in the one over there."

Following his guide, Quincy stared. The older the generations of males in the family, the more sand is on the symbol on their headstone. "Does this happen on the other Brotherhood family graves?"

"Not all the members are buried here in the city. But yes, the few who are do have the same progression of time revealed as less in the hourglass," Marco said. "Do you see how Rick has a countdown of when the fulfillment of reclaiming the silver and names will fall to him?"

Quincy nodded. "But how could they have known the time?" He moved closer to Rick Varela's great-grandfather's headstone and read a weather-worn epitaph out loud. "*Time flows like sand, but he who commands the shadows masters the hour that consumes him.*"

Marco scowled. "Considering the dates on this stone, he wasn't an expert at commanding shadows concerning the hour that consumed him. He died at forty-five years old. Family records only mention that a tragic accident on his sugar plantation in the Caribbean claimed his life, and they sent his body back to St. Augustine."

"Could he have died in a slave uprising?" asked Quincy. "The records Father Morales gave me indicate the Brotherhood was involved in human trafficking."

"Yes, it is, but his family would never admit such an event or such a humiliating death for an elite family lineage," said Marco. "And Quincy, I believe these men each expected to be the ones to recover the silver and the names. They may have been blind to the concept of how much sand was being engraved into their headstones. The dark realm operates in deception."

As Mercedes began receiving photos from Quincy's research, telling her to upload them as evidence into the group's project folder, she gasped. Sonja's head jerked up. "Everything okay?"

"Oh—yeah, just surprising," Mercedes said. Sonja nodded but watched her, and when the photos stopped coming in, Quincy added a text saying he and Marco were on their way back to the condo.

She hesitated, then sent him a message asking if the photos were for the team to see now or later. Quincy told her not to share them yet. He planned to talk about them with the team when he returned.

Mercedes bit her lip, then texted him again. *If I understand this, the Brotherhood had a mission. Every generation passed on a relay baton, and Rick Varela holds it now. Quincy, you must be the one for the appointed time.*

"Tough they do not worship God, the Brotherhood does not deny He exists. They deny his involvement in time, and that is more dangerous," said Father Morales. His low, accented voice came through Quincy's phone speaker as the archaeology team worked at the dining table.

Alex looked up from his notepad. "Wait—how is that more dangerous? God invented time and works in it to bring about His plans in history. Denying that fact places the Brotherhood against Him."

"True. But they don't believe they *oppose* God," Father Morales explained. "The Brotherhood believes God is distant and that earthly time can be manipulated, leveraged through dark forces using secrecy, bloodlines, and obligations. Access to this secret power is only available to a few privileged people, like them. They believe ancient forces are transactional, not sovereign, and those forces govern time and circumstances for now. The inscriptions Quincy saw today aren't correct theology, but they are a signature of secret societies. Sadly, most people in the world who own a Bible know next to nothing about what is inside. They have no defense against societies who frame deception in terms that sound vaguely biblical."

Quincy sighed and sat back in his chair. "The book of Ecclesiastes is about the flow of time, the purpose of human existence, and the human experience. Everything has an appointed time. The Varela headstone implies that a force on his side controls time for the purposes of those who know how to harness that power, and it appoints events and settles accounts. But that's not true. God intervenes in time and sets the rules for the final judgement. Those forces will eventually demand payment for their services—with interest. Each of those headstones represents a human living an eternity of consequences."

"Precisely," said Father Morales. "A reckoning is inescapable except through salvation in Jesus Christ."

"The Brotherhood overlooked Psalm 90," said Mercedes as she looked at the digital Bible on her tablet. "Verse twelve asks God to teach us to number our days carefully so we will develop wisdom in our hearts, and verse seventeen asks for the Lord's favor and to establish the work of our hands. If I understand the theme of the friar's messages and clues, vengeance, greed, and blood stain the hands of generations of men in the Brotherhood. Ancient forces have no need of the power, silver, or the revenge that men valued. The Brotherhood, not the dark powers, was the one who was manipulated."

The team nodded, silent for a few moments as they considered this. Then Father Morales' voice filled the phone speaker. "True. Greed, theft, and blood are indeed the legacy of the members of the Brotherhood of Shadows, and we will find evidence that they silenced truth-tellers like Friar Mateo de la Cruz. In their beliefs, there is no mention of the word evil, and they worship nothing, for that would be a weakness. They believe judgement can be delayed according to their transactions with cosmic bookkeepers—so they pass along revenge in their generations."

Then Father Morales wrapped up his phone call with a statement that gave the team a simple way to think of their mission. "My friends, the Brotherhood believes time hides the truth. Quincy believes time reveals it. That's why they fear him."

After the conversation with Father Morales, Quincy's team cooperated to make dinner and then got back to work on their research. Juana and Marco came in with some dessert and snacks.

Frustration edged Sonja's voice as she gathered her notes on the table in front of her. "What happened—or almost happened—last night is hard to get off my mind. It's a miracle you're alive, Quincy. There's nothing people won't do for money, as the ominous warning on the tombstone proves. If we only knew what the message in the bottle said, we might have the clues we need to unravel the messages about the angel and wings."

Alex pointed at Quincy. "True. That threat about how the Brotherhood won't rest until they reclaim their silver is unnerving, and we won't know what the message in the bottle says for another couple of days. I think Marco is right. Varela will try to get the silver, and you'll get jail time, or an early ticket to heaven. Say we figure out all the clues to find what the friar hid. Before we can get evidence pinning the crime to the Brotherhood, Varela could have thugs ready to take it and Father Morales could accuse us of stealing it."

Mercedes leaned forward, shaking her head. "I understand the concern, and Marco was right to warn us of danger. But don't forget the inscription included the certainty of an appointed time that the silver and the names will be revealed. And that time hasn't happened in almost three hundred and forty years."

She reached for Quincy's hand. "Quincy, you know this is your case to solve, come what may. You know it's time for the truth to come to light; I can see it in your eyes."

The couple looked at one another for a long moment. Quincy's demeanor was resolved.

Alex sighed. "Okay, she's right. And come what may, I'm with you."

Sonja drew a deep breath, then nodded. "I am, too. It's just wise to be honest with each other and consider what we're up against."

Quincy sat back, looking at them each in turn. "At any point, you can either drop from the project or stay behind here at the condo and stick to research. But what happened at the parking lot convinced me that I am supposed to be working on this. Let's get started with what you found today."

From the kitchen area, Juana and Marco overheard Alex say he could not find anywhere in St. Augustine to look for a statue, carving, or painting of the angel Gabriel, nor anywhere with wings that might guard an obscure truth.

Alex clicked his favorite ink pen. "I don't know what we're looking for, but my imagination won't let go of that list of names Friar Mateo de la Cruz left and what Father Morales said about it not being something friars of the time did. The list seemed to contain random saint names, but he made a note beside Gabriel, saying he guards what is hidden. It was an obvious clue. Gabriel is important, and his name shows up in other snippets around the church library."

"What is this about the angel Gabriel?" Juana asked as she went to stand at the table where the team was working.

Quincy decided it was okay to tell her about the clues. "This is among the notes the friar left in the library, and we're trying to establish whether this is a clue that still exists today."

Juana moved to sit on the ottoman near the table. She looked over at Marco, who nodded and took a seat on the sofa.

"Well, my family's old chapel is the Capilla de San Gabriel, with a statue of the angel Gabriel guarding the door since the late 1600s," she said. "It's weather-worn marble, and my ancestors made a cast of it long ago because with every hurricane, we wonder if we will need to replace it. Like the Bible's depiction of him, this angel is powerful and has no wings. He looks like a man, but with unquestionable authority as a messenger from the Lord. Since the passage in the book of Daniel mentions Gabriel flew to him, and in case this is about wings rather than speed, the design of the iron gate to enter the garden is the shape of wings. My ancestor covered both possibilities."

Stunned, the archaeology team stared at the journalist. It was Marco who broke the silence. "Generations of my family have passed down a tradition regarding the chapel and the wings. We have long lost the intention of the saying and assumed it was only meaningful in the past. Each father passed it to his son."

"If it isn't a family secret, can you share with us what the tradition is?" Quincy asked.

Marco hesitated, shrugged, then nodded. "I guess it's okay to tell you now." He said something in Spanish and translated it. *"The wings guard what time has hidden."*

Alex and Sonja both leaned forward, anticipating a revelation about this piece of the puzzle. "Are there any more connections to Gabriel in the area?" Alex asked.

Juana shook her head, her expression skeptical. "I'm not aware of any. I've always assumed the angel was an adopted symbol because of my family's last name, and as for the winged gate, it's a stylized motif with the first letter of my last name in it."

Though no one said her name out loud, it was in everyone's mind. Her last name honored the powerful archangel with the distinction of being one of only two named good angels in the Bible. Among many dispatches the Lord may have sent him on, the recorded ones in scripture were to the prophet Daniel, to Zechariah to announce the miraculous birth of John the Baptist, and to Mary, concerning her miraculous motherhood to Jesus.

Mercedes started searching on her computer tablet for references in the Bible to Gabriel. Alex and Sonja started quick searches for any key references to themes that linked the archangel to the clues that the friar had left behind.

But Quincy remained still, regarding Marco and Juana, who waited for whatever came next. Then, he started leafing through the stack of papers in front of him on the table. He found what he was looking for, and the page swished as he pulled it out and offered it to Juana. "Do you know what this is?"

Puzzled, the journalist studied the image on the paper, turning it around in different ways. With a gasp, she looked at Marco and back to Quincy. "How old is this? It looks like a crudely drawn floor plan, a common layout for small private chapels built as St. Augustine was being settled."

Quincy nodded. "Have you been in a place that looks like that?"

Marco moved close beside Juana to look, and with a start, he pointed out something on the page. "This is the chapel, Juana! The Capilla de San Gabriel."

He looked up at Quincy. "Did the friar draw this? Is this a clue Father Morales gave you?"

"Yes, it is. Juana, if this is your family chapel, is there any reason an arrow is pointing to the door?"

Juana tilted the paper again and squinted. "Oh. I suppose that is an old-fashioned way of drawing an arrow."

Marco pointed something out to her again. "Remember that the statue of Gabriel is over there and that a cross is set into the top of the doorframe?"

She frowned. "But—we've noticed nothing unusual about them." Then she looked back up at Quincy. "I'm guessing you have clues that could apply to the floor plan. That's why it could be important?"

"Yes," he said. "But I need to know if this is the right place. Can my team look at your family garden tomorrow? I know your father is ill. Would this disturb him?"

Juana sat back to collect herself. "We won't disturb my father. He likes to sit in the front window of the house and on the porch in pleasant weather, watching the world and the tourists. You see, we live in the historic district on the southern part of St. George Street. It's a restricted area for traffic, but I will get you access and written permission from my mom to explore the garden. I suppose you will need homeowner approval if you end up digging anything."

Then her expression became wistful. "Oh, how my father would have loved to be part of this mystery, back when he was healthy and aware of his surroundings."

Marco reached over to squeeze her hand, and a look of camaraderie passed between them before he looked up at Quincy. "I can take you there in the morning. But we must be careful. We don't want trouble to follow us to Juana's home."

Chapter 7

It was odd for Mercedes to be riding in Marco's car rather than in the rental truck with Alex and Sonja. The truck was leading them, and an SUV with two security guards brought up the caboose on their little train. She had not texted her mother about the incident with the invisible driver of the stolen car that targeted her and Quincy, but she would let her know there was someone watching them and the detective working arranged extra security.

A glance at Quincy did not reveal his minor injuries, and a bandage covered the scrape on her elbow. He sometimes winced if he turned and his hand darted to his ribs, but it was muscle soreness that would heal soon, according to the emergency room physician.

It was her fiancé's demeanor that had her attention. When he was released from the emergency room two nights ago, he was somber and thoughtful. But after he returned from his outing with Marco the next day, he had been serious and distracted. Alex tried to get him to smile by making clever jokes when he arrived back at the condo, but Quincy barely acknowledged that he had heard him. And after she saw his photos and heard his theories about the Brotherhood's connections to the friar's notes, she understood the danger they could be in. This would weigh heavily on Quincy.

With a sigh, she looked out the window at the sparkling blue water of Matanzas Bay. It looked so peaceful. She wondered why the name had never been changed. After all, the Spanish word for slaughter was not a name for a wonderful tourist destination. Instead, it anchored a horrible historical event to the site. Under the command of Pedro Menendez de Aviles in 1565, the Spanish massacre of French Huguenot forces there secured Spanish control of Florida for about two hundred thirty-five years.

She blinked and jerked her head to look at Marco when his hand-held radio blurted on in the front seat and the voice of the security officer in the car behind them started talking. "You were right. We can't go straight to the address on St. George. We have a tail."

Mercedes and Quincy exchanged glances. Marco looked in his rear-view mirror, meeting Quincy's eyes. Quincy nodded at the question he knew the investigator was asking.

"Roger that," Marco said, unruffled, into the radio. "Plan B is now in play. Quincy, call Alex and let him know."

Quincy was already on his phone, which Alex answered through the speaker in the rental truck. "Plan B?" Alex asked.

"Yep, we've got a tail," Quincy said solemnly.

"No surprise. See you in the parking lot, which is full of driverless cars," Alex quipped. Then he hung up.

Quincy smirked at Alex's joke about the driverless car that someone had sent hurtling toward him two days before. But Mercedes reminded him that Alex is anxious about him being in danger.

"True," Quincy said. "But he's also excited at this turn of events. He loves an Indiana Jones adventure."

From the front seat, Marco snorted. "He should be careful what he wishes for. We're too likely to have one. What's the relationship between him and Sonja?"

"It's complicated," Quincy said with a smile.

Mercedes was more helpful. "It's just my opinion, but I believe Sonja's smart and wants him to know it, thinking it makes her attractive. And it probably does, but Alex feels threatened by her intelligence and drive. She assumes he should be impressed by her ability, but he's not looking for competition."

Quincy turned to her with a grin. "Wow. I've been wondering how to put this situation into perspective. I should have asked you!"

"To be fair, schools and our American entertainment culture have trained Sonja to compete against men—especially white men," Mercedes said.

"Maybe you could talk to her about it," suggested Marco as he turned the car into a parking area behind Alex's truck. "Juana and I noticed the way they look at one another sometimes, and the way he is instinctively protective of her. I don't know, we just think they should try."

"So, are you and Juana a couple?" Mercedes ventured.

Marco grinned. "We grew up knowing each other and recently decided we wanted to give ourselves a chance at being more than friends. We just seem to belong together, and I can't imagine being with anyone else."

The radio blared again with the security officer's voice. "Our tail hesitated at my turn signal, then went past the entrance. He's being sly. I'm guessing he's parking in the closest spot on the street."

Marco nodded as if the officer could see him. "Right. If he's working for Varela, this isn't his first job. Keep your eyes open."

Curly was regretting this job with Varela. He was not told that the archaeological team would be surrounded by security. Even that pesky investigator was involved, waiting on Varela to take the wrong step so he could arrest him. Curly could be caught in a wide net that dragged him into jail. If that happened, he would spill everything he knew about the man.

Quickly, he found a parking space and looked for where the group was most likely to emerge from the parking area they had chosen. Holding his phone to his ear as he walked, he called Varela.

"What's the report?" Varela asked curtly. "You're late."

Curly rounded a street corner and snorted with indignation. "I'm busy, Varela, dodging all the security surrounding Holmwood. This was never part of the deal. What happened?"

Varela's voice was oily. "Well, there was a little warning for him at a local parking lot. No one was hurt much."

Curly cursed. "Who else is working for you? What if we're in the same spot? I'm not goin' down for any crimes, Varela, I told you."

He spotted the archaeology team going toward St. George Street, the main pedestrian mall in St. Augustine, and relief washed over him. The street would be crowded, easier for him to go unnoticed.

Varela's tone was condescending, and it grated on Curly. "Where are you?"

For a fraction of a second, Curly opened his mouth to answer. Then he said, "Looks like we're sightseeing in town today. I'll get back to you."

He hung up before Varela could respond.

Quincy's team put Plan B into play. They wore light backpacks, as did many young tourists in town, and no surveillance would know the contents. Quincy and Mercedes pretended to see something in a shop on St. George Street and asked if Alex and Sonja wanted to go in with them. But Alex and Sonja stood on the sidewalk pretending to consider, and they decided Sonja would meet up with Alex in a nearby hat shop after she went to the public restroom.

Curly hesitated, confronted with the challenge of the group splitting up. The investigator, Marco Alvarez, stayed with the archaeologist, Holmwood. That was predictable. The other security officer stationed himself outside the shop Holmwood's assistant went into, watching the door and the nearby restroom the female assistant went into. He scanned the street and turned his scrutiny onto Curly, though his eyes were not visible through dark sunglasses.

Feigning interest in a sports clothing shop window, Curly casually moved, looking for their reflection in the window. But it was no good. So, he pretended to feel a notification vibration on his phone and pulled it from his pocket. He turned his body enough to see their movements from the corner of his eye.

Inside the store, Alex watched through the large front window from a vantage point where he could not be seen. He noticed the guard keeping an eye on Curly, and when the spy took out his phone, Alex saw it was an older model. Quickly, he texted Quincy. *Ask Marco if I can tag the phone of the guy following us. This is legal.*

Soon Quincy answered. *Marco said yes, keep it within fifty feet. He wants updates if it works. He's impressed you know about public space tracking.*

With a smirk, Alex worked to tag Curly's phone to set up a simple proximity alert. He set his to get a ping whenever the stalker was within fifty feet, per Marco's instructions.

"Can I help you find anything, sir?" asked a young store clerk in a charming Southern drawl.

Alex burst into a big smile, then said, "Yes, as a matter of fact. My friend will be here in a few minutes, and she needs a bandana. Do you have any with a bright tropical print?"

Mercedes did a double take when she glanced at Sonja and Alex. Sonja was wearing a turquoise bandana around her neck—and a big grin. The bandana had neon pink flamingos on it and bright green palm fronds.

As they left the condo that morning, Sonja lamented that she had forgotten to wash her bandanas and had no clean one to wear against the sweat she would deal with in the heat of the Florida sun. Mercedes would have lent her one, but it was too late to go back.

Now, as she and Quincy walked out into the street in different clothing than they had worn when walking in the shop, she could not ask Sonja about the bandana, nor let any sign of recognition pass between them. But the young archaeologist intern always wore boring khaki and tans when working. The tropical-colored bandana not only made Sonja look fetching, but it had also transformed her personality. She was holding Alex's arm and laughing with him as if they were a couple.

Mercedes pretended to aim her camera at a sculpture near them and snapped a quick photo. Then she walked with two other tourists who left the shop when she did. She leaned in to compliment one of them on her unusual purse, hoping the stalker would assume it was a conversation between friends.

Behind her, Quincy left the store with a man he struck up a conversation with while both were buying new Panama hats. He looked different in a fresh shirt and hat, and he paid no attention to Mercedes' group. Marco slipped out the back way and through a shop two doors down to walk up behind them on the street.

The disguises and splitting up to blend with other shoppers and tourists worked, Mercedes noticed with a sigh of relief. She pointed her phone camera at some fun street art in front of her but used the selfie option to look back and saw that the man who had followed them was waiting for them to come out of the store. He took a step forward, then looked torn between waiting or following Alex and Sonja.

She sent the photo to Marco's phone, then took Quincy's cue and ducked into a fudge shop that Marco had entered. The owner allowed them to go out the back door and return to Marco's parked car.

Alex was having fun playing a trick on the man who followed him and Sonja. The spy realized that he lost Quincy, Marco, and Mercedes, and the group had split up. But he would be hoping they would gather again before ending their shopping outing and going out to work.

Every time his phone pinged, he knew the stalker was within fifty feet of him. The security officer with them said he had no criminal record, but he had sometimes been seen with Rick Varela.

Sonja played her role well, pretending to be oblivious to being watched and enjoying her day off from seeking artifacts. As they led the spy on a merry chase, Alex relaxed and let down his boundaries with her. She did not argue when he picked out a fun bandana for her and bought it. Normally, Sonja always wanted to pay her own way and do things herself.

The pop of color around her neck made her approachable, less intimidating, and it brought out the color of her eyes. Something indescribable fluttered in his stomach every time their eyes met. Hers seemed to dance with life and joy that he had not seen there before, and she openly sought to catch and hold his gaze.

Was Sonja pretending to be more than friends for the sake of the man who watched them? Or had she finally let down her barriers, too?

Mercedes did both Sonja's job and her own, taking photos as she approached a beautifully stylized iron gate in Jauna's private family garden. Juana's family had signed an official release with Father Morales. They would allow the garden to be explored and anything of cultural significance relating to a crime in the late 1600s to be removed.

Quincy and Marco unloaded backpacks of equipment, and Juana guided them to enter the park-like area. "My mom will come out later if we find anything," she said. "The less disruptive her absence is to my daddy's routine, the better it is for her."

"It's such a beautiful garden," Mercedes said. She pointed to fancy yellow blooms. "What are these?"

"Oh, those are popular in St. Augustine this time of year," Juana said. "We call them Hurricane Lilies. We have red ones as well. They bloom in August and September, in the height of hurricane season."

"Oh, look, Quincy!" Mercedes exclaimed as Quincy and Marco walked up. "Yellow hibiscus, my favorite, and these are so thick!"

"Our gardener does a great job," said Juana. She turned to Marco and smiled. "And Marco works with him to decide what to plant. The garden has something blooming or thriving all year round. Over there, by the old walls of the garden, we usually have color and keep the shrubbery sculpted rather than making a hedge. We don't want to hide the character of the walls from the early days of St. Augustine."

Standing together, the group enjoyed the view as the low walls led them to the columns at the ironwork of the gate. "It's so serene, and so familiar to me, that it's hard to imagine this gate could be the one the friar's notes mention," Juana said, her brow furrowed. "But what I heard you say about it convinced me that there's nowhere else that fits his description, and there are few places left that date to the time he wrote in."

Quincy and Mercedes opened a folder carrying the copies of Friar Mateo's hints and clues. One page condensed them for easy reference, and they chose it to compare with what they saw in the garden.

"This sketch looks like the gate, without the family initial," Quincy said as he pointed to one note. "*If this message reaches faithful hands, follow the eternal messenger. Enter through the gate where powerful wings guard the truth.*"

Juana scowled. "So—is the truth found at the gate, or by entering it?"

Blowing out a breath while considering this question, Quincy shifted his backpack. "I wish I knew. But entering through it is the first step."

Marco went to the gate with a key, unlocking it and pushing one side open, where a flagstone walkway followed the wall up to the verandah of the house. "I keep the gate and garden maintained, with the help of a friend from church who runs a gardening and landscaping business. We've dug up and replanted many things, but we've never seen evidence of anything buried here."

Mercedes walked through the gate, admiring the beauty of the garden and the old chapel from outside the low wall. Quincy turned around, studying the area inside and outside the gate. Then he said, "Can we see the chapel next? I need to process the setting all together, considering the clues."

The small chapel possessed the aura of the centuries it endured through storms and heat. Awestruck, Mercedes imagined the lifetimes of many people who came and went as this structure served its intended purpose. Graceful blooming vines obeyed hooks up the sides of the stout, aging coquina walls, adding charm without covering the personality of the structure.

But the work of art that riveted her attention was a white marble statue of Gabriel, messenger of the Lord. She appreciated he was depicted as a powerful being who fought battles against evil entities such as the Prince of Persia—not a feminine form with wings. Seen in Bible times, Gabriel was the type of angel before whom humans fainted and were told not to fear.

The voices of the others brought Mercedes back from her thoughts to the work she was doing. "*He who announced the Light of the World points the way to truth,*" Quincy read as he held his page of the friar's clues. Then he looked up and said, "Gabriel came to Mary to announce that she would give birth to Jesus. In the friar's mind, he *announced the Light of the World*."

Wide-eyed, Juana clapped her hand to her mouth. Beside her, Marco almost whispered, "Look, he's pointing to the cross at the top of the arched frame of the door."

In an eager voice, Mercedes said, "This has layers of meaning I want to think about later, but for now, why don't we try to search for a clue at the cross Gabriel is pointing us to? Is there a ladder nearby?"

Marco's eyes lit up at the possibility of finding another lead, and he went to a corner of the garden to a shed for a ladder while Juana unlocked the arched door. "The door had to be replaced over the years, but it's always been replicated in the original heavy Spanish style."

She pushed it open, and Mercedes dreaded the familiar odor of mildew, so common in humid climates. But the chapel was spotless and kept at a consistent humidity to prevent moisture issues.

Marco set up the ladder, and Quincy handed him a few small tools. "You should be the one to find something, if there's anything to discover. Use a file around the cross inset and see if it is hollow."

Marco looked at Juana with a question in his eyes, and she smiled. "Of course it should be you! The Alvarez family has been caretakers of this garden and chapel since the beginning."

The investigator-turned-archaeologist climbed the ladder a few steps up to better see the situation at the top of the door. He studied the cross, then said, "It's set back into a recess made in the same shape. There's no mortar."

"Good!" Quincy said. "But it may still be a challenge to slide it out after so much time. Try to loosen any debris all around it."

Cautiously, Marco slid the file around the cross-shaped stone of weathered marble. Juana jerked back with a little cry when mossy debris fell near her head, and she teased that he had done it on purpose.

Then Marco said he felt the stone coming loose. Carefully, he used Quincy's tools to slide the cross shape out of the doorframe. Quincy moved closer to catch the cross if Marco lost his grip. The ladies waited in hopeful expectation until the item was finally in Marco's hand. Then he studied it and passed it to Quincy.

"You know the clues. Is there anything on this to match your research?" Marco asked.

"Check the carved niche it was resting in," Quincy said. "The cross may have hidden something."

Brows furrowed, Marco leaned closer to the empty, cross-shaped hole in the chapel doorframe. He prodded and scraped with the tools, then heard the clang of metal on metal.

With a quick breath, he glanced at Quincy, who smiled and nodded.

"There's a groove, a crevice, along the back," Marco said as he put his face closer to the space. Carefully, he dragged the long file along until he heard the metal and felt resistance. Working to get one end of the metal object up so he could grasp it, he pulled it from the hiding place.

"It's a key," he exclaimed in triumph, holding it up for the group below to see before descending the ladder. He laid it in his palm and held it out when they gathered around him, then put it into the protective cloth Quincy had in his hand.

"It's greasy," Marco said, and asked Juana for a tissue to wipe his hands.

Quincy studied the old key resting in his palm on conservation cloth. "I'm not an expert in keys, but this is Spanish styling and looks to be wrought iron. There's a bit of pitting, and a flake of corrosion—but if this key is what the friar knew about, or put here, it's in remarkable condition. I believe the coquina and animal tallow—grease—on it preserved it. The lab report will be fascinating."

"Were you looking for a key?" Juana asked, marveling at the iron workmanship. "Does the friar's hint say what this would open? We have all the keys for the chapel, and none are like this."

"My guess is that it opens something that contains silver, or coins," Mercedes offered. "Like a strongbox. That seems to be part of the evidence the friar has hidden. Look," she said, pointing at the page where she had written the friar's clues. "First, we had the map of the floor plan of the chapel, and there was an arrow pointing to the door. So, we started here, with the first clue that Gabriel, the messenger, points to the truth. Christians know the message of the cross is truth, but in context, his clue seemed to make this the first step in a trail to follow, and we found this key. Next, we wrote other clues he gave us in a possible order, and the second one is, *the truth waits for its time where the Word speaks in color*. Maybe this means our next step on the trail is to find something in this chapel or garden that depicts a verse or story from the Bible."

Juana gasped and her hand flew to her heart. She turned a startled look toward Marco. "The stained-glass window!"

"Of course!" Marco exclaimed, following Juana as she hurried into the small chapel. Mercedes' heart pounded as she crossed the threshold into the cool, shadowed interior. Her quick breath was filled with the faint scent of old wood, stone, and candle wax.

The large window rose at the front of the chapel, above the altar. A carved marble plaque beneath it bore a Spanish inscription Juana knew by heart. She brushed her fingers over the worn letters and read softly, "*The Lord God reigns in the appointed end of time*." She glanced at Quincy. "It's our family's reflection on Gabriel's words in Daniel, Chapter 8. The Lord—not human power—will destroy evil."

Quincy dragged his eyes from the art on the window to search for the passage on his phone. Mercedes stepped closer, studying the work of art. Gabriel dominated the center panel as a majestic, radiant figure robed in white opalescent glass. He had no wings, but arcs of gold and pale amber flared behind his head like the first blaze of dawn. His hand reached downward, grasping Daniel's forearm and lifting him from the ground. Behind them was a landscape with a beautiful sky.

Daniel looked upward at the messenger angel with an expression of awe that clutched at Mercedes' heart. His robes were a deep cobalt and violet color, perhaps the artist's idea of what a Babylonian noble would wear.

"Of course he would wear blue," she whispered. "The color of heaven and spirituality."

Around these two figures, the vision given to Daniel unfolded in layers. In the lower corner, barely noticeable, a silver-white ram stood near a winding river of blue-green glass. Opposite it, a dark bronze goat charged forward, its single horn exaggerated and curved. Tiny fragments of amber glass radiated from the broken horn, and farther back four smaller horns rose faintly against a smoky horizon as the kingdoms of men—violent, proud, and fleeting.

Higher in the background, Daniel's other hand clutched a white scroll bound with a crimson seal that gleamed in the light. Beyond it, near the top of the panel, a cross hovered in the sky, formed of white and gold glass. Light gathered there even in shadow, as though the sun waited behind it.

As a thin shaft of afternoon sunlight slipped through the window, color began to awaken in the stained glass. From Gabriel's outstretched hand, a pale beam of gold fell straight downward, illuminating a narrow section of floor just before the altar rail.

Quincy cleared his throat and looked up from his phone screen. "In Chapter 8, Daniel has a bizarre vision he doesn't understand, and Gabriel is sent to explain what the ram and goats with horns mean. Then he gives Daniel God's perspective." He looked down at his online Bible and read aloud in the hush of the chapel.

"Near the end of their kingdoms, when the rebels have reached the full measure of their sin, a ruthless king, skilled in intrigue, will come to the throne. His power will be great, but it will not be his own. He will cause outrageous destruction and succeed in whatever he does... he will even stand against the Prince of princes. Yet he will be broken—not by human hands. The vision of the evenings and the mornings that has been told is true. Now you are to seal up the vision, because it refers to many days in the future."

Silence settled over the group in the chapel. The beasts of glass seemed to recede behind Gabriel's brilliance as the sunrays grew stronger. Daniel was no longer fallen—he was being raised.

Mercedes swallowed, her gaze moving from the sealed scroll to the cross suspended in light. "*The truth waits for its time where the Word speaks in color*," she whispered. "The friar must have been inspired by this silent sermon about time. Daniel fell but was lifted; human kingdoms were raging against Christ, but they were broken; and the message in the scroll was to be sealed for an appointed time in the future."

Marco's voice was almost reverent. "The message about appointed times many days in the future—the friar, he left it for us. I believe Jesus led him to leave this clue to encourage us."

Juana gulped, drew a deep breath, and pressed her hand to her chest. The chapel no longer felt small. It felt watched over.

And as the golden light from Gabriel's hand rested on the strip of stone before the altar, none of them doubted that the Word was still speaking.

Chapter 8

If the couple from the archaeology team and their security guard knew Curly was following them, they pretended not to. It troubled him that there was no reunion with Holmwood for lunch. Holmwood was his assignment, not these two lovebirds flitting about, and apparently, the archaeologist and the other young woman had planned to throw him off and disappear.

He checked his watch again, as if it held the answer to the mystery. Would the archaeologist be at work without his team? Had he tricked Curly? Holmwood's team made the discovery on Treasury Street two days ago, and now he knew why they had not worked in town yesterday. They were spooked by the so-called warning from Varela.

There was a dark-haired, wiry man he did not recognize acting suspiciously nearby as he watched the couple Curly was assigned to. Curly narrowed his eyes behind his sunglasses, then froze as the man casually turned to look right at him. The man's sudden smile was unnerving, knowing, and cruel, and in that instant, Curly had no doubt this man was also working for Varela.

Curly's heart pounded, and he frowned. The man looked away dismissively. Could he be the one who devised the warning that Varela mentioned?

Clenching his jaw, Curly scowled. His role as surveillance for the archaeologists took an instant turn, and he joined the security detail. He moved protectively closer to them and their guard as they wandered down St. George Street.

Quincy's group searched the information on the page of condensed clues and pointed a finger at the words. "There are two here that we thought might refer to the same location."

Mercedes nodded, then read the words to Juana and Marco. "*I did not trust men of shadows; I trusted the rock of sacrifice.*"

She looked up. "The team thinks the reference to sacrifice means an altar of some sort. And the next one seems to be like it: *If justice comes not by the hand of men, let it come where men kneel to find grace.*"

"Men kneel at an altar," mused Marco, then he turned to look again at the shaft of light from Gabriel's hand on the altar area in the chapel. "Could it be here?"

Quincy looked at Juana for approval. "May I search around the altar? I might need to use a file to explore any loose mortar. And I have a device that shows me what's under the floor. It uses radio waves, not radiation or anything harmful. I understand your family originally built this as a mortuary chapel, and the device will not damage the remains.

"Of course," Juana said, almost in a whisper. "If it will not cause damage. But the Gabriel family never used the chapel as a mortuary after all." She kneeled beside Mercedes, who could not resist touching the warmth of cast light on the stone tile. "I wish Daddy could comprehend all this and be out here," she said.

Quincy asked Mercedes for help with the equipment that they needed. Reluctantly, she rose. The colors of light were already shifting. How much time had passed under the powerful message of the stained-glass window?

She had used the new GPR device before but had to look it over to recall how the buttons functioned. This was Alex's job. "Should we check on Alex and Sonja?"

Marco checked his watch. "Security will call me in about fifteen minutes. Is there anything Juana and I can do to help you?"

Quincy glanced up from his exploration of the base of the railing. "Have you ever maintained these supports before? Know of them being replaced or anything? You can check around them and see if anything unusual is present where they are set in the floor."

Mercedes gave the radar device to Quincy, and they examined the stone slabs on the chapel floor. He tapped on the ones in front of the altar, and they both looked up at the same time. Mercedes nodded as he met her eyes. The sound was hollow, and there was no mortar setting the stones in place.

As soon as he scanned the floor, Quincy looked up, startled. He turned off the device, sat down on the floor in front of the stone and covered his face with his hands. The others drew close, concerned. "What is it?" asked Marco. And at that moment, his phone rang.

Sonja edged close to Alex in a restaurant where they had settled for lunch. She pretended to study the menu, but her attention was on the security guard who sat across the table from them.

The guard told Marco they had picked up another trailer and could not shake them. He assured the investigator that he had gotten Alex and Sonja into a crowded place to eat lunch, so their safety was guaranteed for the next hour. "I got his photo and just sent it in to verify his identity. Never seen him around before. The other guy doesn't seem happy about it. Are you planning to come back, or should I call for help?"

Sonja watched while he waited for Marco's response. Alex tried to distract her by asking what she was ordering, so she looked over the menu again.

"Got it," said the security guard. "If they won't take money, tell them I owe them a round of golf next week." He put his phone back in his pocket and turned a confident look across the table to Alex and Sonja.

"Don't worry, we've got this," he said. "Backup is coming from some friends in law enforcement who have a day off. We'll meet them outside after we eat."

Quincy sat on the worn stone floor in Capilla San Gabriel, listening to Marco's conversation about Alex and Sonja with the security officer. "Is there a way to get them here and lose the spies?" he asked when Marco ended the call.

"We can get them to the waterfront and into a waiting car. The stalkers will be on foot and won't be able to follow."

"Let them eat lunch first, but make the arrangements," said Quincy. "I want them here. Father Morales, too. We've found the silver."

Juana gasped and had to sit down. Mercedes beamed at her fiancée and thrust her arms up to heaven.

Marco stood dumbfounded. When he saw Quincy was serious, he stammered, "Are—are you quite certain?"

"Yes. Money and information are all that would be in the strongbox that Friar Mateo de la Cruz led us to," Quincy said.

Marco kept his voice calm as he started making the arrangements to get Alex and Sonja to the garden. Quincy was on his phone, texting Father Morales to meet them.

"Can we use that device you used to find the strongbox over at the wings, at the gate?" asked Juana. "After a break for lunch?"

"I was just going to ask you for permission," Quincy said with a grin. He got up from the floor, dusted off his cargo shorts, and tried to keep his balance as Mercedes wrapped her arms around him.

"I knew it!" she whispered. "Let's go eat our sandwiches, then find what the wings have been guarding."

Rick Varela wore a perplexed expression as he walked out of his office onto the sidewalk, listening to the man he hired to watch Holmwood's team and create havoc if needed. "They are onto us," the man said. "The security guard was reporting to someone, and he herded the couple into a crowded restaurant. Looks like I have a lunch break. Your man Curly is eyeing me while eating a big sandwich."

Varela narrowed his eyes. Curly had not called in since hanging up on him earlier. "No sign of Holmwood?"

"None. He tricked us."

Varela flushed with anger and looked at the bandage on his thumb. He had been so certain of success after all he had done last night. The instructions in the old book were strange, and the steps were intended for more than one person to perform, but surely allowances were made when only one living member of the Brotherhood was left for the ceremony. It was no longer a true brotherhood, with no member brothers around, but his father once told him they remained in brotherhood with the departed ones.

The ceremony had not ended the frightful dream, for it was back when he finally went to bed. He had a lingering headache since waking up and felt off-kilter from lack of a good night's rest.

There was no one else—he must find Holmwood and get the silver! "I'm sending you a number," he said into his phone. "You're on a burner phone, right? Tell the man who answers your call that unless Quincy Holmwood calls me immediately, he won't see his assistants again. They will be pushed in front of a trolley full of tourists."

A harsh laugh crackled through his phone speaker. "That's diabolical, boss, but I'm game. You think they'll believe it?"

Varela smirked. "Most people believe everything they see on the internet, right? And you want the bonus I promised for an accident if necessary."

After ending the call, Varela touched it for another contact. "Councilman Victor Salcedo," came the response.

"Councilman, this is Rick Varela. Do you have any updates on how the project is going with Father Morales and Quincy Holmwood?"

"Hold on a moment, sir. I need to step out of the office," Salcedo said in a mild manner, and the phone went silent.

Varela waited, pacing on the steamy sidewalk. Then the councilman's voice filled his phone with more expression. "The find from two days ago, the bottle found on Treasury Street, is in the conservation lab. There was paper rolled up in it, like a message which might have survived. It can't be unrolled and read until tomorrow. Otherwise, there was no addition from Holmwood yesterday and none reported this morning."

In his mind, Varela turned over again whether the message in the bottle was related to his dream. "What kind of security does the conservation lab have?"

The councilman paused. "Security? Umm, well, I'll need to research that."

"So will I," Varela said, ending the call.

Father Morales was at the winged gate just as the group in Juana's family garden hurried out after a quick lunch. Mercedes stopped short at his expression.

Quincy and Marco reached out to shake his hand before he spoke in a grave tone. "I received a threatening phone call. Your friends are not here?"

Uneasy, Quincy frowned and shook his head. Marco told Father Morales how they kept Varela's men away from Juana's home by leaving Alex and Sonja as decoys. He told him of the plan for getting the couple to the garden soon.

"It is well, then," said Father Morales. "Warn your men not to let anyone near them. I had a call saying unless Quincy calls Rick Varela's number, he will have them pushed in front of a moving trolley, full of tourists."

Everyone stood silent, taken by surprise, uncertain if Morales had said what they thought they had heard. "But—but that's ridiculous!" sputtered Juana. "Why would Rick Varela do such a thing, and why would he implicate himself?"

"Because no one can prove he made the threat," said Marco, irritated. "He uses this signature tactic. Quincy would call him—not the other way around—and he would feign innocence and offer help. Then, he uses connections to trace Quincy's call and locate him. It's all about knowing where Quincy is working."

"Will he do it?" asked Quincy. "Will he really have his man push Alex and Sonja?"

Marco sighed and pulled his phone from his pocket. "Yes, he would, but he doesn't know I have a team of off-duty law enforcement around them right now. I'll make a call."

Mercedes reached out for Quincy's hand. He pulled her to his side, and she felt his tension.

Marco came nearer with his conversation. "You have eyes on both spies, and can buffer them from the couple until the car arrives? Everybody understands the threat?"

As he listened to their assurances, he looked from Quincy to Father Morales. "Do we continue with the original plan? There's no reason for Varela not to carry out the threat, regardless of whether Quincy calls."

"Carry on with the plan," said Father Morales calmly. "We will gather here to pray for their safety. We cannot let this criminal Varela trace Quincy's phone and be led to the San Gabriel home."

Curly followed the young archaeologist couple as they left the restaurant, but he no longer worked for Varela. He was not sure why he felt compelled to hang around, but he stayed closer than before, pretending to look at storefronts, signage, and his phone along the way. The direction they were going kept them on crowded streets toward the waterfront, and he guessed there would be a way of escaping there to whisk them off. Did the other spy expect to see anything different?

Crowds pressed him closer to the road than he had planned. They were making their way to the trolley stop, hoping to get on it before it was full. In the heat of a late summer day such as this, it was inevitable that the odors of human sweat and different deodorants would envelop him, but he stayed, looking for any breaks between groups. He could see one of the security detail men through the people in front of him, but he lost sight of the couple and of the other man working for Varela.

Then the trolley started again, and the tourists slowed down. Curly caught a glimpse of Varela's other spy rushing to the front, close to the young woman with the bright bandana. He bumped hard into a tourist, knocking her shopping bags from her hand, and her companion called out to him to watch where he was going. Curly's adrenaline surged, and he tried to push past tourists to the couple he had watched all morning. He must reach them to warn them!

On tiptoe, he caught a glimpse of the bright bandana and the hat that shielded the fair-skinned young man from too much sun. Beside them, the security guard seemed to have his head on a swivel, watching alertly. His beefy arm reached out, tense and protective, warding off the other spy from reaching the young woman.

Unaware of the chase, the vivacious trolley driver had begun her role as tour guide with a relish, telling the riders about how one of the wealthy railroad tycoons and hotel owners had thwarted the ambitions of another by keeping his furnishings in a warehouse instead of letting them be delivered to St. Augustine by rail.

Then everything seemed to happen at once, and there was a scuffle, a screech of brakes, and screams. More screams erupted from the trolley and bystanders. Curly's heart nearly beat out of his chest, remembering Varela's boast that he had arranged for a warning to Holmwood's team two nights ago.

Marco's phone interrupted the prayers of the archaeological team gathered under a sprawling old oak tree with Father Morales, and he broke his hands from the ring they formed so he could answer. "Yes?"

While he listened, Marco wiped sweat away from his forehead. Sirens blared in the distance, and his eyes scanned the landscape in that direction. "The team is safe? Okay, we're waiting at the garden."

After he ended the call, he turned to the group. "Alex and Sonja are safe and will be here in a few minutes. The guard pushed them into the car before a man rushing toward them shoved a tourist out of his way. The tourist fell to the sidewalk, and the man's momentum carried him over a low planter. Unfortunately, he fell into the path of the trolley. He lost his life."

Mercedes gasped and clapped her hand over her mouth. Juana made a little moan of regret and covered her eyes, and Father Morales crossed himself while saying something under his breath.

Quincy put his arm around Mercedes, asking Marco if the man was working for Varela. Marco said it was one who followed them, and his phone would be checked for the call to Father Morales and Varela.

Then Alex and Sonja rushed up to the winged gate, calling out, and Mercedes ran to hug them.

Chapter 9

The team was together again, shaky, telling their version of being followed and pursued. Alex said, "As long as I felt safe with our security, the chase was exciting, like an adventure—until it wasn't."

Quincy nodded, sighing. "I expected to be the one in danger, not you and Sonja. This is a lesson for me about risking my team's safety."

"Are you kidding me?" asked Sonja. "Juana's family had to be protected. You and Marco had a brilliant plan that led to the discovery you made here, and the one that might remain in the garden for us to find. We were glad to distract Varela's spies, so the team's goal was reached."

"Right!" Alex said. "And we're excited you waited to share the incredible moment when we can uncover what you found in the chapel. Show us what led you there and how we can get it to safety right away. Varela has proven he will stop at nothing, even murder."

Together, Mercedes and Quincy told them how the clues seemed to lead them to the key, the stained-glass window, and the altar. Alex wanted to see the key, then they all went inside the Capilla San Gabriel to uncover the strongbox in the cavity under the floor.

Marco stationed his friends around the garden for security. Mercedes took photos and Sonja recorded video footage as Quincy kneeled before the altar—not in penitence, as people had done here for centuries, but to bring glory to God. If he was indeed the man for this time and purpose, Quincy planned to do his best, and unto the Lord.

Juana had asked her mother to join them while the housekeeper sat with her father during his nap. While her mother watched from a nearby bench in the chapel, Juana moved around, taking her own photos and videos of the work to use for her news report.

Alex squatted across from Quincy, brushing away the dust of many years from the crevices, for there was no mortar sealing them. Marco and Father Morales helped attach large suction grips and move the stone tile partway, enough to peer into the cavity and see what the radar had promised—a large rectangular wooden box with metal fittings.

Dry, cool air escaped from the cavity, smelling faintly of the minerals in the coquina. Father Morales sighed with satisfaction and lifted his hands to heaven. "Praise God, Creator of heaven and earth, whose will it is to answer our prayers by revealing this truth."

The team joined his *amen* together. Then Quincy directed his flashlight to focus on the details of the strongbox. "Whoever built this compartment with coquina knew what they were doing," he said, speaking for the video report. "The strongbox has been preserved in the environment we love to see in Florida. It's dry, stable, and sealed against insects and rodents. The box doesn't look fragile, but it is, and if it contains what we hope, it is heavy. My team doesn't have the expertise or the equipment to lift it intact, so an extraction team is on the way."

He turned off the flashlight and sat back, looking into the camera. "As you can imagine, it will be difficult for us waiting until the conservation lab opens it."

As if on cue for the video, the extraction team started entering the chapel with equipment to lift out the strongbox and take it to the lab. Quincy rose and went to direct them. During the process, he explained each step to Juana and Marco, telling them why they used wedges and slide boards because the handles could snap and the chest could crack, spilling the contents.

The conservation team was professional in its work, and soon the preserved seventeenth-century strongbox rested on a padded board like a stretcher. It groaned a few times as it was lifted by straps, but it held together. Then the lab team wheeled it out to a waiting vehicle.

Juana filmed a short video with her mother standing outside the chapel, near the statue of Gabriel, where she asked her whether the discovery of the artifact would impact her family. "Oh, only in the best way," Juana's mother said. "The box has been here for generations, waiting for God's timing to reveal it. The family had mysterious traditions that referred to it, but the meaning was lost over the centuries. We never owned the contents of the strongbox and were never involved in crimes that may have filled it. Perhaps the first generation of Gabriels gave permission to the friar and Mr. Alvarez to hide the box. But I know this: my husband, and every generation of the Gabriel family, would consider it an honor to have been entrusted to guard this evidence. Now the truth will finally come to light."

Father Morales left with the conservation team, carrying the wrought-iron key Quincy had protected in a cushioned box. They believed it would open the strongbox. He would take charge of the find, protecting Quincy from any accusations of treasure hunting or theft if Varela planned to steal the silver the chest might hold.

Quincy's team watched the van with the priest and the strongbox leave, feeling both elated and deflated. They wanted to know what was inside.

It was Alex who shattered their mood. "So, what was being guarded at the winged gate?"

Mercedes and Quincy looked at each other, smiling, then Quincy turned to Alex. "We haven't solved that mystery yet. Why don't you grab the GPR and let's look?"

Juana was excited as she led them, telling Sonja and Alex they had planned to search at the gate right after lunch. "But Father Morales was there, telling us about the threat he got on the phone, and the danger for you made us forget all else. We gathered to pray for your safety, and soon you arrived."

Alex and Quincy prepared the scanning device while Marco scrutinized the area. "Are we looking for another strongbox?" he asked.

"Honestly, we don't know what we're looking for," Mercedes said. "Your family tradition said that the wings guard what time has hidden. Our only clues are the friar's message that tells the faithful to enter through the gate where Gabriels's wings guard the truth, and the message on the Varela headstones about silver and names that belong to them."

"There may be clues or messages in the bottle we located, or in the strongbox, but we have next to nothing as clues right now," said Quincy. He went to stand at the gate, studying the pillars that supported the heavy iron wings.

Juana's fingertips trailed along the low wall. "Marco and I used to play on the wall as kids," she mused. Then she turned to smile at her mother. "Remember how you kept telling Daddy we were going to fall and get hurt someday?"

Marco laughed. "But we never did, save for a few scrapes." He looked back over the gate and the wall. "Even then, I felt driven to find something weighty here. I yearned to know what great truth the wings guarded, what my family had failed to discover over generations of being caretakers of this garden."

"Quincy, Marco—come look at this!" Alex interrupted. He scanned a handheld device over one pillar at the gate.

Jogging to Alex, Marco reached him first. Alex held the radar and told him to look at the screen. Quincy came beside them and interpreted the image for Marco.

The ladies all gathered around them then, and Marco said, "Are you telling me there's a hollow place in the pillar?"

"Yes, and there's something in it," said Alex. "I believe it is a jar. A big one."

Juana came to take Marco's hand. "Behind that engraved stone plaque? How can we get to it?"

Her mother stepped forward. "Quincy, do whatever it takes to learn whether the jar provides evidence of the crime. The Gabriels do not own what you are looking for, though it might appear we do because of the premises. Justice is the priority here, and there may be an antiquity find of cultural significance for the city and for the state. If you must damage the column, we will restore it. My husband and I discussed replacing that plaque with a new one a couple of years ago, while he could still decide things like that. We never got around to it. What good is a sign with words no one can read?"

"Thank you, Mama," said Juana, and the team also expressed its thanks. Quincy said he hoped they could get to the jar without permanent damage to the plaque, as they had left the chapel just as it was before they searched, minus the hidden object.

Mercedes ran her fingertips over the surface, trying to feel the grooves. "Is this in Spanish?" she asked.

Juana left Marco's side and went to the column, pouring some water from her bottle on the plaque. "Yes. It's easier to see if it is wet. When I was little, I memorized the Spanish words that sounded like a song. My friends all spoke English, so it felt like a little secret in my garden."

She traced her finger over the inscription. "It means, *In memory and vigilance, Chapel of Saint Gabriel, 1688.*"

"Wait—the chapel was new in 1688?" asked Sonja. "I didn't see that in my research."

"The friar could have been seen here as if providing guidance or blessing, and no one would think twice about questioning his presence," said Mercedes. "If he was helping the man who turned in the evidence against the Brotherhood, as we suspect, there was no safer place against suspicion."

"It was private property, so it may not have been recorded on town records," Marco said. "I remember Juana singing about the rest of the words, but she never said the last line."

"I didn't understand the end, and it didn't seem to fit the rest," Juana said. "I liked that no shadows could enter where the wings guarded us. I imagined that my home was like holy ground, sheltered by the Lord, and now I'm convinced that this was true. In English, the rest of the inscription says, *Where the messenger spreads his wings, the shadow may not enter.* I loved it."

"What part didn't you understand?" asked Mercedes, squinting at the plaque.

"*The truth rests beneath faithful wings until time demands an account*," Juana translated.

Marco and Quincy locked eyes, remembering the Varela headstone at the cemetery. *Time will settle the account.*

Quincy's phone rang as the group stared into the space in the winged gate column. He tore his eyes from the sight to deal with the unwelcome intrusion, but his face changed when he saw who was calling. "Father Morales, I was just going to update you on the search in the garden," he said. "I'm ready to send you a photo. Are you free now to return?"

Glowing rays of a late afternoon seemed to set the mossy oaks and majestic palm trees on fire in the garden setting of the Capilla de San Gabriel. Mercedes and Sonja recorded images of the team's discovery as they waited for Father Marco and an expert from the conservation laboratory. Alex made notes, and Quincy went online to compare the findings with similar ones. Marco rearranged his security with fresh volunteers, and Juana and her mother went inside to get refreshments for the team until they had time for dinner.

When Father Morales saw the sealed terracotta jar resting in a cubby of the column, he did not attempt to hide his emotional reaction. Tears filled his eyes, and he gratefully took a tissue from Mercedes. He attempted to speak, but his voice was too choked to be understood.

When he regained his composure, he tried again. Hoarsely, he said, "I can't tell you how shocked I was when I saw the picture you sent, and now, being in the presence of this—this message left for us, I feel as if Friar Mateo de la Cruz left something of himself here. And in a way, this is true. I have not told you that the friar was a skilled potter because it did not seem important in the scope of the clues he left. It was common in those times for friars to have useful trades, and records show Mateo made containers used in everyday service in the mission."

He blew his nose again and took a ragged breath before he continued. "I feel kinship with Friar Mateo de la Cruz, because I sensed from his records that a righteous man risked his life, struggling against the odds to leave evidence for future justice. It is not the spirit of the friar, of course, but the Lord, who is present with us, raining down His incredible blessing at this important event. I am an old man, sometimes inclined to flights of fancy about things I learn in my work in the archives."

"Then Friar Mateo knew well the preservation qualities of fired clay, and what to seal the lid with," said Quincy. "When we found this jar, I marveled at his choice of containers for information so important that he called it 'the truth' in his clues. In this climate, in his time, I can't think of a better way to have stored something to preserve and hide it indefinitely. And if our suspicion is correct, that it contains 'names' the Brotherhood wanted to keep secret, this jar is almost perfect for containing a ledger from that time. It was common to remove books from the covers and roll them for storage, and this one is just the right size."

"I wish we could be alone," Quincy whispered into Mercedes' ear. "Marco is savage."

Beside him on the balcony of the vacation condo, Mercedes suppressed a giggle. "Why do you think he allowed us to step out onto the balcony? This is all the privacy we get until the news is reporting on the discoveries of the Memento Mori Project. He's doing his job."

Quincy's boldness was palpable tonight, and she, too, felt a sense of elation from the day's achievements. She allowed herself to melt closer to his body as he pulled her into a tight embrace. His muscles felt tense, and his heart pounded as he buried his face in her hair. He whispered, "Let's plan a wedding."

Mercedes smiled. His mouth was moving to her face to kiss her cheek gently, but he did not move away as he always did. She felt his indecision as his lips inched closer to hers. Her love and attraction for him surged, but so did caution.

"I never work on wedding plans on an empty stomach," she whispered, and she felt his surprised reaction before he chuckled and pulled back.

"Should I go urge Juana and Sonja to hurry with dinner?" he quipped. Their eyes met in laughter, but then their gazes turned to longing.

The sliding door made a metallic sound as Alex pulled it back to announce that their celebration dinner was ready. The aroma of seasoned steak wafted from inside, and Mercedes looked to Alex as she took Quincy's arm to go indoors. "It smells wonderful."

Rick Varela was shaky as he ended a call with Curly, who gave him what he said was his last report. He would not work surveillance again, he claimed, for Varela or anyone else. Curly had no proof that Varela was behind what happened when his other spy met with a tragic public end, but being linked to an attempted murder was disturbing to Varela.

There was no immediate replacement for Curly, and Varela regretted losing him. He had proven himself to be a professional, though he could not track where Holmwood had been all day.

The local news reports and social media were full of speculation about why a man who was killed after falling into the path of a trolley was rushing and pushing through the crowd. Some agreed with what Curly told him. The spy was making an ill-fated attempt to reach someone for an unknown reason, since no one claimed to have any connections with him. But Curly said the target was the young couple on Holmwood's team, whose security protection put them in a car that sped off seconds before the murder attempt.

Varela turned to stare out of his office window. The councilman had called and reported that there were two deliveries to the local conservation laboratory that created excitement. Father Morales was on hand both times, but the councilman had no one on the inside to feed him information about the artifacts being examined.

This meant only one thing—Holmwood had been digging. He tricked Varela and fulfilled the mission Morales had given him. Holmwood would be famous, wealthier than ever, and in the history books. His name would be on the tongues of tour guides who led groups all over St. Augustine.

Varela could not portray the young archaeologist as a cocky treasure hunter looking for fame and glory. Holmwood was a worthy adversary who had covered his bases, getting the finds into the hands of the next person in the chain of custody. There was no solid ground for accusing him of theft or of staging a remarkable find.

With a sigh, Varela brought both hands to his face. Where had his plan gone wrong? Holmwood should have been the perfect stooge in a set trap to snatch the silver and the names.

Plunking down in his desk chair, Varela's gaze landed on a framed award for his real estate development company. The stylized artwork of the hourglass looked smart and sophisticated. But it sent a sudden chill over him. His eyes did not see the abstract logo but the inspiration for it. The one in the special room in his basement, where he had tried to follow the instructions in the old handwritten book, passed down into his family for generations.

Beads of sweat formed on his brow, and he felt more trickle down his ribs. The antiquated instructions were difficult to read and understand. He had to make a few substitutions for things that no longer existed, or that he could not legally get. He had shed some of his own blood as a sacrifice. But the serpent had not come alive on the hourglass as the ritual instructions promised.

Still, the power that served his ancestors was there; he felt it. It was the power that would serve him, as the last member of the Brotherhood, in his mission to reclaim the riches of the silver and to burn the evidence that would ruin his family's reputation for all time.

It was the appointed time to reclaim what had been taken. He was the one to put everything right again and gain the reward.

He would find a way into that conservation lab, using a link to get access to information about the buildings in the city. First, he would create a distraction to discredit Holmwood. As he pulled up several fake social media profiles that he used to influence local news, real estate, and development issues, he settled on a message and typed it.

In the seventeenth century, British pirates pillaged and burned St. Augustine, terrorizing the early citizens. Today, British pirate Lord Holmwood is pillaging St. Augustine once again and plans false accusations to disrupt our history and damage the reputations of our upstanding citizens.

It was impossible not to notice the warm interactions between Alex and Sonja as Quincy's team, Marco, and Juana gathered in the dining room of his condo over a home-cooked dinner. Juana was emotional about the artifacts of evidence protected on her family's property for so many years. She had contacted her pastor to ask about organizing a prayer walk around the conservation lab that night, hoping to shield it from any attempts at theft. The pastor knew she was not free to share anything about the vulnerability on the site, but he had seen the security guards stationed at the lab and knew there was a reason.

Sonja sat back in her chair and said, "I admit, even though I knew we might be in danger if we were successful, it shook me up to live under security guards. But when that spooky driverless car came rolling toward Quincy the other night, and especially when the man following us today died trying to harm us, things got real. I'm grateful to Father Morales for getting the funding to hire so much security, and to your friends, Marco, for showing up today."

Alex nodded at Marco and reached out to pat Sonja's hand to comfort her. Mercedes' heart warmed to see them together, but then she remembered the danger they had been in. "I can't get a passage in the Bible out of my mind about that man at the trolley," she said. "I looked it up on the way home. It's in Psalm 7, about a man falling into a pit of his own making, and his violence coming back on his own head."

Quincy swallowed a bite of his steak and said, "I immediately thought of one when we heard the news, too. It's about the wicked falling into their own nets while I pass by in safety. There are other verses in Psalms and Proverbs about that theme. But I wish the man today had not died. I pray no one else is harmed during this project."

Marco was solemn as he leaned closer to the table. "If it doesn't crumble, the message in the bottle will be read tomorrow. The lab is small, and Quincy is the only one allowed in with Father Morales, so the rest of the team must stay here. Because of the two threats to your lives, we simply can't risk having you all waiting on the premises. I'm sorry. The work has been a team effort."

He rubbed his temples in weariness before he spoke again. "I confess the tragedy today in town caught me off guard. We don't have any eyes on Varela. He may take the messages on his family headstones as a personal mission, and he can find out if anything was delivered to the lab today. He might act out of desperation to get his hands on the evidence we found."

"We've been careful to keep today's discoveries a secret," Juana told the team. "No one knows about the deliveries to the conservation lab but the employees, Father Morales, and us. None of us has told anyone, not even family, except for my mom, who promised not to even tell my father. Yet the council members could be aware that the contents of the bottle found on Treasury Street will be opened tomorrow. That was public."

Marco nodded. "Yes, and anyone on the historical committees and councils can be in contact with the lab employees about other work, so they could learn there are new additions urgently waiting to be handled. Father Morales has already delayed his schedule to be here this week and needs to travel back to Spain. Even passers-by will notice the extra security on the premises, and anyone gathered there for prayer walks."

Alex scowled. "What must Rick Varela be thinking tonight?"

Mercedes replied, "Whatever the dark power behind the Brotherhood of Shadows directs him to think. *That's* who we're up against—not Varela."

Quincy drew a deep breath to steady his heartbeat as he followed Father Morales into the conservation suite where the contents of the message in the green bottle waited to be seen. The humidity chamber glowed with soft, indirect light, and what he hoped was the friar's letter lay curled on a sterile sheet of mesh. The fibers were finally relaxed enough to manipulate, gently and safely.

A different technician was on duty today, the supervisor in charge of the lab. He greeted them, wearing a magnifying visor, and beside him, an assistant smiled and waited.

The technician said. "I know you are anxious to see what we have here, so let's not delay. The parchment wrapper should be pliable now."

He glanced over at his assistant, who confirmed that the humidity was fifty-eight percent. Father Morales stood watching, his hands pressed together almost as if in prayer, while the technician handled the roll through the chamber gloves.

Tiny flakes of salt and aged fiber drifted free when the outer parchment was loosened with a micro-spatula under one edge. Through a microphone on his collar, the man said, "The outer parchment is free and responding. Now, I'll be easing it off the paper."

Quincy knew this process would be done millimeter by millimeter, but he still felt tension building in his neck and shoulders and tried shrugging to ease it. The parchment fell away like a discarded cocoon sooner than he expected, revealing a faint, uneven linen rag edge that must be the paper the friar wrote on. It was pale and stiff.

The conservation expert focused on his work and nodded to the assistant as she reported the status of the humidity. He placed two damp blotter strips nearby, and the humidity in the chamber rose to sixty. Speaking into the microphone recorder, he reported on his next steps while he coaxed one edge of the paper with tweezers dipped in silicone.

Quincy stopped himself from stepping closer when he saw a corner unfurl and reveal ink. He knew how to do this, but it was not his lab. He stared with excitement at the iron gall ink, dark and ready to speak after over three centuries.

The assistant recorded video and photos of each stage of the exposure of the text as the lines appeared slowly, reversed in the relaxing curl. When the sheet lay open, weighted down by inert rods, the technician announced with a hint of triumph that the document was safely open and could be read. "Father Morales, this is written in Old Spanish. Would you step closer and translate, or examine the photos for a good look?"

The archivist eagerly came closer. As his eyes moved over the elegant, deliberate handwriting, he stopped and murmured a prayer. He glanced at Quincy and brushed away tears. In a broken voice, he said, "I'm sorry, I'm overcome. A moment, please."

Quincy bowed his head, thanking the Lord for this discovery and asking Him to prepare his mind and heart for what he would learn. He prayed for continued protection from those who would not want this information to be known.

"To his most Catholic Majesty, our Lord and Sovereign, King Charles II of Spain, Keeper of the Faith, Defender of Christendom," came the Father's accented voice. Quincy's head shot up, and he listened to the style of writing from another century, feeling eerily as if he were in a dream.

"From the least of your servants, Fray Mateo de la Cruz, of the order of Saint Francis, resident in the mission at San Augustin

in la Florida." Father Morales translated as he read, then he paused, taking in the message's importance.

Everyone in the room listened in hushed reverence. Every sentence had the effect of a door opening to another world, another time, people who had lived before them.

Father Morales' voice grew stronger, as if he were a herald delivering the letter to the king. *"May Your Majesty receive these lines with the charity and patience you extend to all who labor for the Crown. With a trembling hand, I set forth grave matters, compelled by conscience and duty before God. In the course of hearing confessions from a most tormented soul—an accountant of the Treasury for this province—I was made privy to sins that cry out to Heaven for justice. He revealed to me that certain members of the town council, entrusted as stewards of Your Majesty's revenues, have diverted gold and silver from the royal accounts. Not only was the treasury defrauded, but much of this wealth was employed in a commerce most vile: the unlawful trafficking of men and women stolen from their homes, who are bought and sold in secret contrary to both divine law and the ordinances of the crown."*

Quincy's stomach tightened, and he felt a flash of disgust. In his mind, he envisioned a mafia of sorts committing these crimes. It was too common throughout history.

"The confessor, in anguish, entrusted me to a chest of coin and record, begging that it be sent in silence to Your Majesty as proof of the corruption," Morales continued. *"Yet before he could be absolved and protected, wicked men, fearing exposure, cut short his life. Fearing for my own, and discerning shadows at my steps, I write swiftly in hope of reaching a loyal officer bound for Spain. Should this letter come safely into Your Majesty's*

august hands, I beseech that justice be wrought upon a company of men calling themselves The Brotherhood of Shadow, who have committed treason against the Crown. A repentant accountant, Alonzo Alvarez, placed into my hands a chest of silver belonging to the crown, along with his ledger. The ledger bears the names of influential men and the sums stolen over several years."

Father Morales brushed his hand across his eyes. He looked up at the others in the lab. "I feel a shadow of the weight of fear and responsibility the friar must have experienced."

Quincy nodded his understanding. How many times had he felt the same way on an excavation site? The technician and the assistant waited, spellbound but respectful of the need for a break.

Then, the archivist waved a hand and cleared his throat, looking back at the centuries-old letter to a Spanish king. *"I believe my life is in danger. I have hidden the chest and ledger where no man of impure heart will easily find them. Whether this letter reaches Your Majesty, I cannot know, but I entrust it to Providence. If I perish, may these words be my testimony: that I sought to serve truth and righteousness, and to preserve the souls of those who sinned against the Lord and Your Majesty. May God keep you for many years. I remain, though unworthy, your humble son in Christ and servant of the Crown, Fray Mateo de la Cruz, Mission of San Augustin, La Florida, In the Year of our Lord 1688."*

With the closing words of the letter, only the soft hum of the humidity chamber and the soft whisper of the air-conditioning vent broke the stillness. After a few moments, Father Morales said, "The friar wasn't just afraid for his life. He felt the burden of having hidden proof of treason, a chest of silver and a ledger. No wonder he left frantic clues; clues he hoped an evil man could never understand."

He turned to the technician. "You may say this bottle has been opened and contained a brief document dating to the Renaissance era, and you can report on its remarkable condition. But the contents of this letter must be secret for now while we work on the other two discoveries we have made. I do not exaggerate when I say this is a matter of life and death and could mean danger for the lab employees. Two more days. Do you understand?"

Chapter 10

Quincy's team was whisked away from St. Augustine when he and Marco returned from the conservation lab. Juana warned Father Morales of the false accusations circulating among local social media users, though community history enthusiasts could not find the source of the rumors about an archaeologist named Lord Holmwood and whether there was any truth to the posts. Some scorned the theatrics of the statement; others wondered if there was an element of truth about genuine discoveries wrapped in the dramatic description. No one had yet linked Quincy's website to the posts because he never referred to himself as being titled.

Though Father Morales used no social media, as an archivist he understood how news spread. He contacted his superiors to find the source and to handle any damage if there was a link made to the church. Then he implemented the arrangements he had made for this scenario. The safety of the archaeology team was his first concern.

Once he reported to his superiors about the incredible significance of the letter he had read in the laboratory, he had permission to do whatever was necessary to keep both the discoveries in the lab and the team who recovered them safe.

For the archaeologists, this move to another location was unsettling. None of the team members were sure how to update their families about progress on the project, or whether the social media speculation would reach beyond St. Augustine.

After dinner at a Christian retreat center where they would stay for the night, Mercedes and Quincy escaped the stress by walking to the seaside. They rocked gently in a double swing, watching the surf massage the sugary sand. The soft breeze, the cry of gulls, and the whispering small waves soothed their hearts.

"Quincy, will you call Zeke for me tonight?" Mercedes asked, stroking his arm. "I don't know how to tell my family why we are here today. He will."

Quincy nodded. "Yes. It feels so strange, not being able to share what we found. All I can say is, we discovered a letter that confirms what we believe we have recovered, but we can't prove it for two more days. I texted that much to my dad, fearing he would get calls about being Lord Holmwood. People trying to figure this out might wonder if he's the archaeologist involved. The use of social media for sensation and disruption irritated him, but he handled it well. I could hear the excitement in his voice. He needs to work again in the field, here in the States."

An early moon sailed over clouds tinted in the colors of twilight. Mercedes gazed at them. "Maybe that's something to consider in the future, Quincy. You could work together again."

Stretching and yawning, Quincy smiled, then draped his arm around her on the back of the swing. "Maybe. My mind is so overwhelmed right now. All I want to think about is us. In a way, I wish I'd done as you planned, taking time off to pull a wedding together and start our future. It can't be as dangerous as this."

Mercedes feigned shock. "And miss making one of the most mysterious historical discoveries ever in the oldest city in America? Ghost tours out by the Varela family graves at the cemetery will make this one a hit. You're tired and not thinking straight. Besides, friends tell me I haven't experienced stress until I plan a wedding."

He turned to her with a lazy smile, and the sea breeze stirred his brown hair. She felt a strange longing to freeze the moment, to memorize it—to stop the sands of time from slipping through the cosmic hourglass.

Quincy read her eyes and knew her heart. He leaned closer, then sighed when he heard Alex's voice. "Hey, lovebirds, we need to talk about something."

Mercedes's eyes sparkled with laughter as Quincy's look held them. Then he surrendered to the interruption and sat back. "This had better be important, Alex," he growled.

Alex waved his faded beach blanket like a flag before it rested on the smooth sand in front of them. "Oh, it is. You should know this before you go back inside and see Marco."

Sonja sat down on a fantastical steampunk mechanical fish, and Alex sat cross-legged beside her on an underwater mechanical vehicle.

Quincy looked curiously at Alex, and Mercedes raised her brows at the proximity of Alex and Sonja together on his long-used beach blanket. They were certainly more comfortable with one another.

"Yeah, Father Morales wanted to prepare Marco for the possibility that the Alonzo Alverez in the friar's letter was an ancestor," Alex said. "Good thing he did, because Marco recognizes the name from family traditions and is pulling together some puzzle pieces in his mind."

Mercedes put her hand to her lips. Wide-eyed, she stared at Alex and then at Sonja, who nodded that he was telling the truth.

"Father Morales is making many connections, as well, with the Alvarez stewardship of Juana's family garden and chapel," Alex continued solemnly. "This was like a pact made between the two families to guard the evidence until the time it would be discovered."

"Marco isn't upset, just overwhelmed," Sonja said. "Can you imagine his feelings about faithfully keeping the family tradition of helping care for the garden, gate, and chapel, not understanding why, and then learning he protected the proof of a crime his ancestor confessed to being part of, but hid the evidence for, waiting on justice?"

Quincy closed his eyes and sighed. Beside him, Mercedes said, "This is incredible! Look what Jesus did—Juana and Marco contacted Quincy about working together on this project with no idea they had a generational stake in the investigation!"

Sonja nodded and said, "Wait until you hear this! Marco said, *my family and the friar didn't mean these things to be secrets forever. Only until the right man arrived to reveal the truth.*"

"How does Juana feel about all this?" Mercedes asked. "Just think of how many generations of both families were involved in preserving this evidence. Can Father Morales arrange for some compensation to the family for their service?"

"Ten to twelve generations," Quincy said. "And Father Morales is working on compensation. I wondered when I heard the contents of the friar's letter this morning whether there was a connection with the Alvarez family, because of the traditions about wings guarding the truth. Who would care about the truth except for one who wanted it to be told? If Alonzo Alvarez is Marco's ancestor, more evidence about him will come out when we open the strongbox and the jar. I'm glad Marco is prepared, since Juana has exclusivity on the news story."

"Oh, that's not even everything Father Morales told Marco," Sonja said. "He understands because he, too, had an ancestor involved with the Brotherhood. Like Alonzo Alvarez, Morales' ancestor stumbled into the knowledge of their crimes and circumstantially became linked enough to be entangled in human trafficking. He wasn't in St. Augustine as a citizen; he served on a Spanish ship in port here for a time. He sent a letter home asking for help with his dilemma with a friend on a ship leaving sooner than his own, because his life was threatened."

Alex elaborated. "In those days, you know, second sons didn't inherit the estates, and some found another way to make a living. Morales' ancestor was the first son; the younger brother went off to become a soldier, though he didn't need to. When his brother was murdered, Morales' ancestor was outraged. He started a relentless investigation that every generation picked up, to no avail, due to lack of evidence such as what the friar left behind. Father Morales trained in the church specifically to find the archives about the Brotherhood and waited for the role here to come around."

Sonja and Alex looked expectantly at Quincy to show surprise. Mercedes did, but Quincy sat calmly beside her, nodding. "Yes, now that he's revealed this, I can tell you he disclosed his connection on the day he asked me to take the job. If the Morales name appears on documents or the ledger, he wanted me to know he had never been involved with the Brotherhood of Shadows."

Alex shook his head, smiling. "I knew you were sitting on information you couldn't share with the team."

Beside him, Sonja looked off into the dunes, her thoughts far away. Then she said, "All this stuff about generations following traditions, protecting truth, and seeking justice—it's so out of touch with modern culture. Most of my friends are like me, without two parents in their home, or they cope with the stress of blended family situations that aren't like-minded. They get sent off for a weekend with another parent and their new date or spouse, or they don't even know where one parent is. I know the historical perspective on the *Memento Mori* project, and I see the proof we discovered, but honestly, if I told my friends about it, they could never relate to the stability of Juana and Marco's lives. For that matter, they would not relate to Rick Varela's life, anchoring himself to a centuries-old group his ancestors belonged to."

Mercedes and Quincy exchanged glances while Alex reached for Sonja's hand. The beach was bathed in last-light while each of them explored their own thoughts. Then Quincy said, "I'll be honest, Sonja, Mercedes and I grew up in families with generational histories, and hers involved a crime—a murder. If you ever want to know our personal stories about how it ended this summer, we'll share them any time. Just as in the project our team is working on, our stories are much like Juana and Marco's. So, we can't claim to know how it feels to be in most modern families. But we, too, have many friends like you, and we're good listeners."

Smiling weakly, Sonja brushed away an errant tear. "I want to hear all about it when this project is over."

Mercedes sat bolt upright, jerked from a deep sleep in a room she shared with Sonja and Juana at the retreat center. Juana was already moving, pulling on a sweatshirt over the tank top she slept in and grabbing her Glock from her bedside table before going to find out who was pounding on the door.

"Who is it?" Juana shouted impatiently.

Mercedes' bare feet hit the floor, and she stuffed her arms through the sleeves of a jean shirt to cover her pajama top. Sonja sat up, dazed from a deep sleep.

"It's me," said Alex, his voice muffled through the door. "There's been an emergency."

Recognizing his voice, Juana lowered her weapon and unbolted the door. "What's happening? Do we need to get dressed?"

"Yes," Alex said. "We might have to return to St. Augustine. We didn't want to wake you, but the news keeps getting worse."

Juana nodded. "Okay, we'll be out soon. Where do we meet you?"

"The lobby on this floor. Hurry!" Alex said, and he turned to jog down the hall.

Mercedes heard distant voices until Juana closed the door and rushed to get her clothes on. Sonja yawned but said nothing as she stumbled out of bed and reached for the shorts and tee shirt she had thrown on a nearby wooden chair. Mercedes hurried to the bathroom and reached for the hanger with her clothes for the next day. They quickly took turns washing their faces, brushing their teeth, and untangling their hair.

Mercedes hastened her steps to follow Juana down the gloomy hallway to the lamplight of the lobby. There were no other visitors on this floor, and the dark night surrounded them through the windows, hushed and surreal.

She squinted and blinked in the lamplight. A large monitor screen in the lobby assaulted her sleepy eyes. Quincy looked up and came to take her hand. "Come on, sit over here until your eyes adjust and you're coherent," he whispered, leading her. "I just got hot lemon herbal tea for you in the kitchen, and a chunk of your darkest chocolate bar to wake you up."

Alex was waiting for Sonja with hot chocolate, and Marco led Juana to a steaming cup of the same tea Mercedes had. The men's efforts to provide comfort struck Mercedes as odd, and she became alert and uneasy. Something was very, very wrong.

Father Morales came from the kitchen that opened into the lobby, twisting the cap from a bottle of water and looking troubled. He nodded to Alex, who was connecting his laptop to the monitor on the wall. His thick accent added to the bizarre setting. "I'm sorry to wake everyone. But my security team at the conservation lab alerted me to trouble. There's a chance we must return."

Mercedes braced herself for the inevitability of bad news. The citrus aroma of the herbal tea soothed her as she closed her eyes against the world and took a sip. The sweet taste of honey comforted her, as did the warmth of the mug she cupped in her hands.

Alex connected his laptop and looked up at the priest. Father Morales nodded, and Alex pressed something on his keyboard.

A news reporter sprang onto the screen. He pointed behind himself to live video footage of flashing lights and law enforcement vehicles.

Juana gasped at the alarming presence around the familiar building. She almost spilled her tea as she hurried to set down her cup and get out her journalist's notebook.

"We know one perpetrator escaped, and both sustained wounds," said the local news reporter. "The other is being transported to a hospital. Another crime that took place at the same time is being investigated. A man allegedly threw unknown objects at a local church, shattering windows and leaving a suspicious package near them. He started a fire and ran from the scene. When a passer-by saw it, he used an extinguisher from his truck, so it caused minor damage. Law enforcement has had a busy night covering both crimes."

The news coverage went to a commercial, and Alex scrambled to find more live coverage on the internet. Father Morales said, "The distraction divided my security team. One had to leave at the end of his shift and the other one stayed, waiting for the next shift to arrive. But the incident held the fresh guards up in traffic at the church. As you can see, the distraction was too perfect to be unplanned. The conservation lab was vulnerable with only one tired security officer."

When the screen came to life again, a reporter was on the scene. "Security cameras at the facility were not functioning at the time of the break-in." News cameras panned the building and found gold when a police officer moved away from examining blood smears on the outside wall.

Mercedes groaned and turned to Quincy. "Varela?" she whispered.

"Councilman Victor Salcedo," said Father Morales. His face and tone were grave.

Juana gulped. "Please tell me no one from my church was there praying."

"No, it was after midnight," Marco said. "Only the security guard was there, just as the thieves planned. Two men in ski masks knocked him out from behind, rendering him unconscious as they disconnected the alarms and broke in. But the security guards who got delayed found a detour and arrived. They realized what was happening and called for the police and an ambulance as they went in for the thieves, who were armed and threatened them. One panicked and took a shot at the guards, then he ran. The other took a shot before escaping out another door. They returned fire. Outside, the same thing was playing out as two police officers arrived on the scene."

"Did they damage or steal anything?" Sonja asked.

"They had no time," Alex said.

"It is unclear whether there was a getaway vehicle near the scene," the reporter said into the camera. "A search is being conducted, and local businesses and residents should be alert for an armed and dangerous man in the vicinity near the lab. He has injuries."

While the news displayed maps of the area, Father Morales' phone rang. He walked outside to speak to the caller, and Alex muted the volume on the monitor.

"Oh, Quincy," said Mercedes, wincing.

He pulled her to his side to relax against the back of the sofa. She realized he had said nothing and showed no surprise at the crime. "Varela had to get the silver and the names,

Mercedes," he said. "It was his time, just as it was mine and Marco's."

Rick Varela gasped for air, half-running, half-lurching along a planned route to the nearby cemetery. The silver and the names were not with him, to be buried with the black hourglass in the family plot. No one would expect such a hiding place.

Without the strongbox, he had no use for the transportation that he and Salcedo had arranged for. The distraction in town had not been enough to delay law enforcement or the next shift of security guards.

It would be okay. Salcedo was likely dead. And if he survived, he could not prove Rick was his accomplice. There was no security footage.

He stumbled among tombstones and monuments to find the Varela family plot in the moonlight. Anyone who suspected him of being part of the break-in at the conservation lab would look at his home or office, not in the cemetery. It was safe here.

The headstones, large and small, leaning or new, radiated with an eerily bluish glow in the moonlight. When he recognized the shapes of the headstones at his family plot, he sprawled on the ground, panting for breath and reeling from pain. Adrenaline got him here, but agony was his world now. Perhaps he would pass out. It would be a mercy.

But an elderly man, clearly wealthy, appeared nearby. He wore linen and silk made in another era. One gnarled hand was holding the hourglass of the Brotherhood, and almost every grain of black sand filled the bottom. A golden serpent coiled around the waist of the glass, glittering in the moonlight as it slithered off the edge and to the ground, moving toward Rick. The ghostly man's other hand disappeared into an old strongbox, like pirates once used.

He turned from looking into the box to meet Varela's horrified stare. The face was familiar, like an old portrait he had seen in yellowed albums, and the skin was like parchment that had been crumpled and smoothed out again. But the eyes were terrifying, black voids of eternal darkness.

The apparition lifted his gnarled hand from the empty box. There were no coins, as in the other nightmares, because the time to reclaim them had run out. The gnarled, skeletal hand pointed at him in condemnation, and the awful visage wore no grin this time.

The conservation lab hummed with the low, steady whir of the air control system that maintained the range necessary to open, study, and preserve artifacts. The old strongbox Quincy's team found under the floor before the altar at Capilla de San Gabriel sat at the center of an examination table, resting in its custom foam cradle. Quincy felt the familiar thrill that came when he was about to discover long-hidden secrets.

The lab technician held up the heavy iron key Marco had discovered for the video recording, then she inserted it into the lock. They were all surprised when the key slid in with a soft click.

Then the sound of a deep inner bolt shifted for the first time since the late seventeenth century. The technician paused, then turned the key slowly. Metal whispered on metal, and the lock surrendered to the mechanism.

For the benefit of the recording device, the technician said, "Opening now."

With steady hands, she tried lifting the lid. It resisted, but her training had taught her patience. It rose, and Quincy wondered if he imagined a sound like a sigh and a puff of air that lifted like a spirit.

How could he help but drop his jaw at the sight of the contents in the box? It was clear from the technician's expression that she had seen nothing like it. Quincy looked for Father Morales' reaction and knew he restrained himself from moving closer.

On the very top of everything rested a clay tablet, inscribed and lying on a linen cloth, stiffened with age.

Of course, Quincy said to himself. *A message that would stand the test of time.* Aloud, he said, "Father Morales, can you translate it?"

"It's fired clay, handmade by a potter," the technician said. "This is completely stable; the message I wish we would find more of! I'll lift it out."

Once the tablet slid off spatulas onto a padded tray, the technician nodded to Father Morales. He cleared his throat and began reading in his thick accent.

"I, Fray Mateo de la Cruz, servant of Our Lord, set down these words upon clay, that this witness may endure. This coffer was entrusted to my keeping by a man whose conscience became aligned with God's. He prayed this be returned to His Majesty, but his voice was silenced by men of darkness on that very night. Pray God that whosoever finds this will not covet it but deliver it

into just hands. The hourglass empties by the will of the Almighty, not by the shadows who mean to control it. Judgement draws nigh. I write quickly, for evil men's eyes are ever upon me. May Christ preserve the one who finds this from greed and fear. The legal record is guarded by angel wings. Deo Gloria."

Quincy locked eyes with Father Morales. "The information in the clay jar."

The technician took her place at the strongbox, where the contents were no longer obscured by the tablet. With gloved hands, she moved coins around to examine them. "Gentlemen, the lab will count these for an exact inventory, but the coins on top are pieces of eight stamped with the Pillars of Hercules and the shield of Castile. Would you like me to move on to the clay jar now?"

Mercedes, Sonja, Alex, and Juana waited in the garden around the chapel, where the sculpture of Gabriel pointed at the cross. Mercedes took a seat in the small chapel, admiring the stained-glass window whose colors had rested on the place where they found the strongbox. Gabriel's interpretation of Daniel's vision, created three centuries ago, reminded people that important prophecies still awaited fulfillment. God's word would come to pass in His time.

Her joy over the justice from their recent discoveries mixed with sadness. Councilman Salcedo had recovered enough to learn he may not survive his wounds, so he confessed his plot with Rick Varela to steal and share the contents of the discovered strongbox.

She left the quiet coolness of the chapel when she heard Quincy's voice out in the garden. He was in the shade of the sprawling oak, where the team gathered to hear about the artifacts in the lab.

Quincy described his experience and promised to share photos of the messages the friar had written. Not only had he preserved a letter in clay inside the strongbox, but he had also preserved in the clay pottery a ledger Alonzo Alvarez had given him, dated 1688.

"My ancestor's name appeared in the ledger as a bookkeeper, not in any illegal transactions," Marco said. "Father Morales' ancestor did not appear by name. But Morales pinpointed the transaction date when a group was paid. It matched the date in his family's records for the deed that his ancestor was in trouble for, and he found a later transaction for payment made to the murderer. He is relieved to have closure to this mystery in the family history."

Alex wanted details about the ledger. Quincy said, "It was about thirteen inches tall, nine inches wide, and an inch and a half thick. The book was filled with rag paper, sewn, and he removed the stiff covers so it would roll up."

Quincy used hand gestures to explain how the ledger was preserved. "The friar waxed a sheet of parchment in the friary's own beeswax and wrapped the rag paper ledger in it to repel moisture. Since he was a potter, he used his own wide-mouthed jar to stuff the package into. As you saw when we found it, he put the clay lid on top. Sealing it made it airtight."

"I guess this means Juana has her news about the Memento Mori project," Sonja said, touching Juana's arm. "And the end of this adventure has meant so much closure for both your families."

Marco smiled. "Yes, and we can't thank you enough. But Memento Mori was a more appropriate name for this than your team realized. They discovered Rick Varela."

Mercedes first felt relief, then dread, connecting *memento mori* to the news. *Remember, you must die.*

Alex made the same connection. "So, where was he?"

Quincy said, "After Marco gave the police a tip, they found him in his family's gravesite. An antique wrought-iron hourglass was lying next to him. The glass was shattered, and the black sand had all spilled out."

Marco said, "The security team believed they had shot him at the lab. Adrenaline must have surged because he ran to the cemetery, then collapsed and bled out from his wounds. We captured the man who started the commotion at the church, and he was supposed to pick up the councilman and Varela, helping them with the strongbox and taking it to be buried at the gravesite. Now Rick Varela's will be the last of the family burials."

Her voice was almost a whisper when Mercedes looked at Quincy and asked, "Was the metal serpent found in the shattered glass?"

He shook his head. "No. The friar drew it as if it existed, like the Brotherhood members did. But if it was real, it has disappeared."

Mercedes and Quincy stretched out onto two poolside lounge chairs at her cottage in Bluffton. The evening was tiptoeing to the coastal town with a glorious display of color above them, and a soft breeze blew from the May River. "When the summer is over, I'm going to miss this, I won't lie," Mercedes said lazily.

"Hmmm. Me, too," said Quincy. "Let's spend the weekend doing nothing but enjoying time together."

After a few moments of companionable silence, Quincy said, "I got a text from Alex. He is visiting Sonja and her mother for a few days."

"Do you think it helped her to talk to us about our family stories on our last night in St. Augustine?" asked Mercedes.

"Alex claims it did. He said she's changed a lot since the day they misled the surveillance and pretended to be a couple. Trying on that role seemed to have opened a door for them to make it real, and the reality of being in grave danger in St. Augustine that day changed her priorities about how she valued time. His understanding and patience about the pain she is working through from her family situation sealed the deal for her. She said that's what love looks like."

Mercedes sighed. "Oh, Quincy, how amazing! Despite the deaths and drama that occurred during the work for Father Morales, there was so much healing and now a new relationship. I think Alex is just the guy to be Sonja's white knight—second to Jesus, of course!"

Quincy laughed. "I love the way you framed all that happened. Have you thought about the card Juana and Marco wrote the note on, with the early wedding gift they gave us? I keep thinking about the sentiment. *Time relentlessly moves on. Things change. People change. But truth never changes, and we must seek it as we build the foundations for our lives.*"

Mercedes rolled over onto her side to look at him. "It stuck with me, too Quincy. Our friends and family slip into eternity, and few of us leave evidence that we were here. Yet it matters a great deal how we lived. As the Bible says, we must not be weary in doing what is right."

Quincy mused, "In my line of work, I've seen many treasures corrode and crumble. They lose the meaning they once had after a thousand yesterdays have quickly gone."

Mercedes leaned closer to him and kissed his ear. "Yesterday's pass, but you and I should be thinking of our tomorrows. Only the Lord knows how many we have, but I plan to show and tell you about my love for you in all of them."

Did you like this novel? You can continue the adventures of Mercedes Ellison in the Strange Sands Series. Remember to help other readers by sharing your review!

There is a list of **Resources** for readers who enjoyed this novella series and want to investigate certain aspects of it. For Book Clubs, there is a page called **Discussion Topics** to help leaders guide conversations and glean more spiritual insight from the stories.

Stay updated with me via my fun-packed author newsletter and websites at Southern Sky Publishing[1] and Pamela Poole Fine Art[2], or join me on YouTube[3], Goodreads[4] and BookBub[5].

1. http://www.southernskypublishing.com
2. http://www.pamelapoole.com
3. https://www.youtube.com/channel/UC9aV3zHRlASXUUBEF7xbT9Q
4. https://www.goodreads.com/author/show/3934732.Pamela_Poole
5. https://www.bookbub.com/profile/pamela-poole

Resources

There are so many! This one is where I find the most helpful research material for both reliable, quick references and for in-depth Bible Study, Biblical Worldview writing, and research for archaeology and history in this book.

YouTube has many podcast interviews and conference presentations with the late Dr. Michael S. Heiser about the Bible, but those who want to dig deeper will discover a lot of extra material and primary sources on this scholar's main website. I highly recommend his book *Supernatural* and his videos on the Divine Council and Cosmic Geography:
Dr. Michael S. Heiser[6]

Others:
Alicia Childers (former Zoe Girl singer)
Melissa Dougherty (author of Happy Lies)
Iron and Myth (Derek Gilbert)
Creation Ministries International (History, Science and Archaeology)

Archaeology:
Using GPRS in Archaeology, https://www.geophysical.com/using-ground-penetrating-radar-archaeological-sites

History of St. Augustine
https://www.citystaug.com/693/Our-History

6. https://drmsh.com/

For Book Club Discussion

Can you think of examples of how an event in the past is revealed and how it sheds new light on previous beliefs and situations?

There are many times in the Bible when truths await an appointed time to be revealed. Look up examples and discuss whether those have come to pass or will be known in the future.

Some Christians feel a strong attraction to follow a direction in life, and they believe the Lord is guiding that path. Has there been a time when you were convinced you were being led to an opportunity to serve Jesus? What happened?

About the Author

Inspiring Southern Fiction

Pamela Poole writes inspirational mystery and suspense that explore the intersection of faith, history, and the unseen spiritual realm. Her stories are grounded in a clear Christian worldview and shaped by a deep respect for both historical preservation and biblical truth.

Pamela writes inspirational stories that bring together Christian faith, historic places, and hidden truths. Her novels reveal how the past can press into the present, where faith becomes essential to discernment and courage. Her characters are ordinary people facing extraordinary challenges, learning to trust Jesus when darkness threatens and answers are not easily found.

Pamela is the author of the Strange Sands Suspense series and the Painter Place Saga, blending richly detailed settings with themes of calling, obedience, redemption, and spiritual warfare. Her fiction offers clean, thought-provoking suspense designed both to engage the imagination and to encourage the heart.

When she isn't writing, Pamela enjoys research, painting in her art studio and on location along the Southern coast and making memories with her family and friends.

Readers and art enthusiasts alike can enjoy her YouTube channel[7] for painting demos and art education presentations. To enjoy the latest content, sign up for her

7. https://www.youtube.com/channel/UC9aV3zHRlASXUUBEF7xbT9Q

fun-filled newsletters and follow Pamela Poole Fine Art[8] and Southern Sky Publishing[9].

8. https://www.pamelapoole.com/

9. https://www.southernskypublishing.com/

More Books in the Strange Sands Suspense Series

The Old Cedar Chest, Strange Sands Suspense 1

Hilton Head

An antique cedar hope chest. A hidden document. A century-spanning vendetta.

The Old Cedar Chest launches a faith-filled suspense novella series following architectural historian Mercedes Annalee Ellison as she uncovers the unexplainable forces tied to historic properties—and her own family legacy.

Mercedes never expected her great-great-grandaunt's fragile journal and a tattered manila envelope to change her life. Yet the miraculous way they came into her possession—and the unease they stir in her spirit—would give even the most hardened skeptic pause.

Before she can meet her first client or settle into what she hopes will be a quiet summer at a Lowcountry cottage, an ominous shadow stretches across her carefully planned future. Mercedes soon realizes she is the target of a vendetta that goes back more than a century. Time is running out, and survival may mean accepting a calling she never sought and a destiny bound to the legendary Ellison family.

In this heart-pounding Christian suspense novella, Mercedes must rely on more than her education and instincts. Anchored in faith and surrounded by eerie revelations, she learns God equips ordinary people to stand firm against extraordinary challenges. Filled with mystery, history, and spiritual depth, The Old Cedar Chest invites readers to consider how faith, courage, and divine purpose intersect in life's unseen battles.

The Hidden Hallway, Strange Sands Suspense 2
Savannah

An antebellum house. A hidden hallway. A tale of passion and revenge.

In *The Hidden Hallway*, architectural historian Mercedes Annalee Ellison faces another assignment that challenges not only her professional expertise but her spiritual resolve.

Tammy and Clayton Popplewell hired Mercedes as they registered and renovated an antebellum house in the beautiful Southern city of Savannah, Georgia. But she knows this is not the boring job she hoped for when she arrives on the first day to find the local police there. What should have been a routine assessment of aging blueprints and structural quirks takes a chilling turn when Mercedes uncovers a concealed hallway that doesn't appear on any original plans.

As Mercedes investigates the history of the property, she must rely not only on professional skills but on God's guidance to discern something hidden—and why it matters now. When neighbors seek her out with a strange Civil War Era tale of passion and revenge, she works to uncover a terrifying darkness and help her clients make the house into the inn where they dream of sharing light—before they give up and she loses the job.

The Hidden Hallway is a gripping Christian inspirational suspense novella blending history, mystery, and spiritual warfare. Set against the rich atmosphere of historic Savannah, it's a story of faith tested, dreams endangered, and the assurance that God is always present—especially where secrets hide.

The Freedom Staircase, Strange Sands Suspense 3

Charleston

An enduring plantation. A legendary patriot refuge. A last stand for freedom.

It thrilled Mercedes Ellison to be chosen to work as an architectural historian for Majestic Oaks, a plantation that endured and survived wars on American soil. The stately Georgian mansion features the Freedom Staircase, where legendary patriots stopped for refuge in their roles with the Continental Army in the American Revolution. Her client needs help to keep the plantation he inherited, which is steeped in the history of the Lowcountry of South Carolina, home of the Swamp Fox and four signers of the Declaration of Independence.

There are also some unsolved mysteries on the property. Bringing them to light will help her client, and she finds clues in a secret passage used by the patriots. But then her archenemy dies in jail, and his son watches her. The long-standing vendetta against the Ellison family that began in *The Old Cedar Chest* now escalates, and Mercedes knows the danger she faces is real, personal, and relentless. Can she make a last stand for freedom from the past that began with the murder of her ancestor on a stormy night in England?

Blending historical intrigue, Christian faith, and suspense, *The Freedom Staircase* is an inspirational story of legacy, obedience, and the courage to walk the path God sets before us, even when it leads straight through danger.

The Dark Passage, Strange Sands Suspense 4
Bluffton

Faith tested.
Purpose questioned.
Evil revealed.

Mercedes Ellison is hoping for a quiet summer as she plans her wedding—boring clients, simple renovations, no surprises. But the Marlowe House is anything but ordinary.

Doran Marlowe, a former missionary guide, has spent decades traveling the world's most remote regions. His shuttered passageway and unsettling artwork hint at experiences he never fully left behind. His sister, Mary Lou, newly returned from the mission field, carries her own burdens—discouragement, doubt, and unanswered questions about her calling.

When a terrifying incident shatters the calm of the historic home, Mercedes finds herself drawn into a mystery that defies logic and explanation. The danger feels personal, spiritual, and disturbingly familiar.

In *The Dark Passage*, Pamela Poole weaves a faith-filled suspense story that confronts spiritual darkness with biblical truth. This inspirational mystery asks hard questions about obedience, spiritual authority, and trusting God when the unseen world breaks into the ordinary.

The Devil's Drawer, Strange Sands Suspense 5
Beaufort

An ominous oath taken for personal privilege.
An enigmatic artifact unbound by time and place.
An evil consequence for generations.

A chilling mystery unfolds at Seashell Cottage as architectural historian Mercedes Ellison stumbles upon an ominous black cabinet decorated with ancient Egyptian symbols. Delivered under the cover of darkness, this enigmatic artifact pulls her and her client into a web of secrets that stretches across generations.

As they delve deeper, a private investigator friend joins them in unraveling the sinister connection between the cabinet and a long-buried family oath to a clandestine society. With blood as the ultimate spiritual currency, they must confront the haunting legacy of a deceased ancestor whose evil choices ripple through time, binding Mercedes' client in ways they never imagined.

This gripping story is filled with suspense, intrigue, and revelations. As a Christian, Mercedes knows that Jesus reverses curses. But will her client come to know this before it is too late?

Other Books by Pamela Poole
Southern Sky Publishing[10]

The Painter Place Saga
Painter Place
Hugo
Jaguar
Landmark

3 Legends of Painter Place (short stories)
The Wind Songs of the Marsh
King's Ransom
The Castaway and the Mermaid

Southern Sky Devotional
Inspired Artistry—Embracing the Creative Calling

10. https://www.southernskypublishing.com/

www.ingramcontent.com/pod-product-compliance
Lightning Source LLC
LaVergne TN
LVHW090950080826
845145LV00003B/958

* 9 7 8 1 9 5 6 0 8 9 3 3 2 *